HIS COUNTERFEIT CAMPFIRE BRIDE

Camp Firefly Falls, Book Two

GWEN HAYES

This is a work of fiction. Similarities to real people, places, or events are entirely coincidental.

HIS COUNTERFEIT CAMPFIRE BRIDE

**First edition. July 2016.
ISBN-13:
978-1535092203**

**ISBN-10:
1535092203**

Copyright © 2016 Gwen Hayes.
Written by Gwen Hayes.

For Johnny and Frances

CHAPTER ONE

Well, hell. She's wearing the pencil skirt again.

Of course she was.

Miguel Castillo paused at her open office door. Not to leer. Not exactly.

Well, yes, exactly that.

Most of the time, his feelings for Ms. Seraphina Worth ran pretty cold, much like the lady herself. But on pencil skirt day, he encountered a swift and unwelcome temperature change.

Generally speaking, Miguel preferred blondes. Tall blondes. Tall blondes who surf, if he were given a choice.

Sera was none of those things.

She was petite. Like she might break into pieces petite. And she was brunette, which was fine, but she would never surf. Not in this lifetime. She wasn't outdoorsy. She didn't …muss. He liked women not afraid to get a little dirty—in bed and out. Sera seemed more like the lights out, missionary style, once on Saturday nights to get it over with kind of girl.

But when she wore the pencil skirt, it was always with the damned red lipstick.

He was screwed.

She still hadn't noticed him as she looked out her window and talked into her phone. The sunlight streaming through the blinds landed on her, and he was shocked that he felt it in his gut. He was not allowed to have those kinds of feelings for Sera Worth. It was unprofessional and impossible. She was his co-director. She was his nemesis. And she was so fucking annoying.

As if she heard his thoughts, she cocked her head and met his gaze, raising her eyebrow. Just one. One perfect arch over the rim of the reading glasses she must have forgotten to take off when she answered her phone.

"I'll call you back, Phillip," she said into her phone. But she was looking at Miguel. And what she was saying was, "What do *you* want?"

Before the race for the promotion, they'd gotten along for the most part. Mostly because they ignored each other. She wasn't on his radar then—unless it was pencil skirt day, of course. And life had been fine.

But then the director position opened up and things got…mean.

They both wanted the job. She probably wanted it more than he had, at first. But the way she kept harping on him about not being the man for the job—Well, it had rankled. Miguel was not the most mature man he knew. When someone challenged him the way she did, continued to do, he couldn't just laugh it off. He had to win. He had to conquer. He had to beat his chest and go primal.

And then he got mean, too. It was like a horrible political campaign during election year the way they threw each other under the bus whenever they could. Lines were drawn and blithely ignored. Co-workers were dragged into the muck. Toward the end, he wasn't even sure he knew himself anymore, but he knew for damned sure that Martin & Lewis Group would be fools to hire either one of them for the job.

And surprise…Mr. Martin decided to do them one better—he gave the job to both of them. A shared position. Neither of them lost…but neither of them won, and it was a daily struggle to find a place to put all his caveman feelings.

What was worse was that he now had a job he hadn't really wanted, still didn't really want, and it came with extra responsibilities. Miguel wasn't irresponsible, despite what Ms. Worth had said about him to anyone who would listen all those months ago. He just didn't care for being overly burdened with obligation. He enjoyed the feeling of a job well done—but that was about as far as it went. Sera, on the other hand, seemed to revel in the glorious importance of her duty.

She finally noticed she was still wearing the reading glasses and slid them off her nose while she walked to her desk. "Hello, Miguel. Do we have a meeting on the calendar?" she asked primly. Again, it meant, "What *do* you want?"

"I just wanted to see if you'd had a chance to look over the focus group file."

She nodded, and how she managed to make even a head nod look condescending, he didn't know. "Let's do a quick meeting after lunch?"

Of course. "Another meeting? Can't we just talk about it now? I'm right here. You're right here. Why do we have to plan to meet when we can just do it?"

Her dead-eye stare was more potent than an eye roll. She had perfected her brand for sure. Ice Princess. "I want to finalize my notes."

Advertising pitches weren't meant to be done in the middle of the day over a clean desk. Advertising was about all-nighters and too much coffee. It was about white boards and on-the-fly ideas. It was the adrenaline rush of near miss deadlines that kept him at his optimum performance level. And he performed really well for Martin & Lewis Group.

Miguel stepped all the way into her office. "Why can't we just *talk*. Brainstorming is not a four letter word. In fact, it's a staple of our profession. I'm guessing you've heard of it."

Oh shit. Her hands moved to her hips. That meant he was about to get *schooled*. Which was bad enough. But getting schooled by her in that outfit, with that lipstick, was something he was not supposed to enjoy. Yet, he felt his interest rising, the flow of adrenaline beginning. He wanted to roll up his sleeves. Dig in. Get them both mussed.

"I do brainstorm. I just like to do it on paper, alone with my own thoughts. Your way is not the only way."

"Neither is yours, princess."

The sound of someone clearing his throat behind him stopped her from responding to Miguel and instead she said, "Mr. Martin."

"In my office. Both of you. Now."

MR. MARTIN PIVOTED AND WAS out the door before Sera could respond.

So she sent Miguel a "what is going on?" look. Because if he knew something and hadn't told her…

He shook his head. And luckily for him, looked just as confused as she felt. "I have a feeling this is not good." He stepped back and gestured her to the door.

She hated that Miguel was always a gentleman. Jerks should not also be gentlemen. But he never failed to open her door or push in her chair. It wasn't out of the realm of possibility that he was doing it to piss her off. But it was also just as likely that he was simply raised well. He had his share of negative traits, but his manners didn't make the list.

The walk down the hall was a long one. She focused on her breathing. It was important to still her emotions. Not get anxious.

Count to ten, Sera.

She wondered how many times she'd counted to ten in her lifetime. It was a trick the therapist taught her when she was eight years old before her surgery when she'd just been diagnosed for the second time in her young life with coarctation of the aorta. Quite a mouthful for a kid. Everything had gone topsy-turvy in her life, and she'd had to learn too early how to manage stress. The therapist taught her how to focus on the things that were in her control and how not to obsess about whatever wasn't in that circle.

It's possible that counting to ten was an outdated tactic and there were better ways of dealing with her feelings now that she was an adult, but it still worked and she had no desire to mess with it at this point.

The last six months, though, she wouldn't be surprised if she'd counted to one million in increments of ten. Something about Miguel Castillo brought out her need for counting. A lot.

On the surface, he was Mr. Fun. Everyone in the office loved Miguel. He didn't put on airs or drive a flashy car. He was just six feet of yummy tanned skin with the requisite dark hair and eyes. He laughed a lot, and the lines around his eyes were a sexy testament to that.

But underneath the surface, he lived to make her life unbearable.

Yes, she was controlling at times. Yes, she supposed it could be annoying. But she didn't have the luxury of just "letting it happen." If she'd *let it happen*, she'd have died before her tenth birthday. Nobody in her life, certainly not her mother, had been mature enough to make sure the meds didn't get mixed up or appointments didn't get missed. Sera had to organize her own pills and study city bus schedules and routes to the clinic. She'd learned how to find books in the library about congenital heart defects. How to ask doctors the right questions. How to keep at the doctors and nurses until they answered her, even if she was just a child.

So, yes. Sera took things seriously. Everything. Her health most of all. And that meant knowing what was and wasn't in her control, and controlling the hell out of the things that were.

Her job: in her control. Her co-director: so not.

After insisting that they both sit, Mr. Martin drummed his fingers on the desk in front of him without saying a word. For an interminable amount of minutes. A thousand times she wanted to say something, anything, and ask what he needed to see them about. Break the tension as it ratcheted higher and higher. But she sat with her hands folded primly in her lap and waited him out. She was surprised Miguel chose a similar tactic, though his body was more or less sprawled in the chair.

They waited.

And waited.

The ticking of the wall clock getting louder. The silence bearing down, pressing against her skull like the atmosphere right before a rainstorm. She concentrated on her breathing. She concentrated on Miguel's shoelace. She tried to clear her head. She—

"Do you know why I promoted you both to director last month?" Mr. Martin startled her out of her intense study of a carpet divot.

She and Miguel exchanged a glance.

You answer.

No, you.

He shook his head. She narrowed her eyes.

Mr. Martin exhaled loudly. "Because you two were supposed to be my dream team. You both had qualities I wanted for the position. You were *both* perfect for the job. So what could be more perfect than having you both?" He paused long enough to take a breath, but not long enough for anyone to answer the rhetorical question. "Except you're not. Together you are useless."

"Mr. Martin—"

"I mean it. You haven't brought me a damn thing I can use, your staff is afraid of you, and HR says someone has complained about a hostile work environment."

That brought Miguel up from his indolent slouch. "A hostile work environment? That's insane."

Mr. Martin raised his hands in front of him. "I assumed that there might be a few bumps to smooth out, but I had faith that the two of you could make it work. You're my superstars. But neither of you can figure out how to compromise and you're not bringing down my entire company to play your little ego games."

"Mr. Martin—"

He shut her up with a look. "I am giving you one last chance."

Her heart rate slowed again. Okay. She wasn't sunk.

He slid two envelopes to them across his desk. "You are going on a mandatory business trip. Tomorrow. For one week."

"Tomorrow?" Miguel asked while she opened up the envelope. Plane tickets and a packing list for…summer camp? "For a whole week?"

"What is Camp Firefly Falls?" she asked as she scanned the list. Bug spray and flashlights? She'd never been camping in her life.

Mr. Martin smiled. Not a very nice one either.

"It's a summer camp for adults. They run different themes all summer. You two are going to the team building session. You will come back with whatever certificate they award, and if there are ribbons or awards or competitions, you will work together to win every single one of them as a team. If you don't come back with proof that you can not only work together, but are the best damned team since Captain and Tennille, don't come back."

Who were Captain and Tennille?

Miguel scraped his hands over his jaw. "Team building like...walk across hot coals and fall into each other's arms stuff?"

Mr. Martin answered with a shrug. "I really don't know what they do and I really don't care. All I know is that you will find a way to win and you will find a way to work together or you won't have jobs to come back to."

"But our accounts—" They couldn't just leave for a week.

'Your first task is to delegate. There isn't any wi-fi at summer camp."

"What?" they both shouted at the same time.

"The brochure said cell service is spotty also. Good luck. See you in a week."

They'd been dismissed. They looked at each other and back at Mr. Martin, but he was already rounding the desk and striding out of his own office. Leaving them there.

"This is ridiculous," Miguel said. "He can't just send us to summer camp. We're not twelve."

"I can't lose this job." She hadn't meant to say it out loud. She knew better than to show weakness in front of Miguel.

But her mom...she could *not* lose this job. There was no way she could cover two mortgages while unemployed.

He leaned forward, hands on his knees, and stared at the floor. "Nobody is losing their job. If you weren't so..."

Rage exploded bright red behind her eyes. "Are you kidding me right now? This is not my fault."

"All I'm saying is that…hell, I don't know what I'm saying. We don't have much choice. We'll go to summer camp and we'll come back with a bunch of blue ribbons for three-legged races and best s'more makers. We don't have a choice."

"Agreed."

They both blinked at the idea that they could agree on something. Anything. Because for six months, they hadn't been able to agree on anything as simple as *What is today's date?*

Miguel let out a strangled laugh. "See, Ms. Worth? It's already working."

CHAPTER TWO

Welcome to Camp Firefly Falls
Are you ready for the time of your life?

From the Activities Coordinator:

Established in 1971, Camp Firefly Falls was a popular family retreat until the late '90s, eventually closing in 2000. It was purchased two years ago by the Tullys, who renovated the ghost camp into a getaway for adult campers seeking to escape the mundane and retreat to a simpler time—only this time the liquor runs freely at your new favorite all-inclusive resort.

Your cabins have bathrooms and maid service every day. Water toys, canoes, sports equipment, kayaks, and beach towels can be checked out at the boathouse and are included in your stay. If you should need any amenities, please visit the lodge and we'll try to accommodate you.

Please read and abide by all rules and regulations included in your packet. (There are not that many and they are there for your safety.)

First Day Schedule
10:00-6:00 Registration
10:00-6:00 Tours every half hour. Meet at the tennis courts located on your map.
5:00 Cocktail reception in the boathouse
6:00-7:30 Dinner
9:00-2:00 a.m. Campfire

MIGUEL DIDN'T QUITE KNOW WHAT to make of coldhearted Sera Worth wearing shorts and a ponytail. He sort of assumed she slept in her business suits and pencil skirts. If he had imagined her in shorts, they would have been longer. Ironed probably. The cut-off denim was a big surprise. Not a welcome one. He didn't like that she could surprise him. He didn't like that she looked really good in Daisy Dukes. He didn't like that her legs were curvy and strong and that he wasn't the only one who noticed. But there she was, standing in front of him in the long registration line at Camp Firefly Falls.

Jesus. Summer camp.

He did feel twelve again, actually. And it wasn't the worst feeling in the world. From where they stood, he could see cabins in the distance, lots of playing fields, even more trees, and a lake peeking through a break in the pines. He heard someone say zip-lining…and he'd put money down that most of the guys in this line would play a pick-up game of ball without hesitation. If he just kept a good attitude, this could be like a vacation. There were plenty of women in line. Gorgeous women. His type of women. He didn't need to obsess about his business partner's curves.

But there was a guy a few people ahead of them who was also obsessing about his business partner. And Miguel added one more thing to his list of things he didn't like. Him. Preppy, bland, and exactly the type of guy she went for. Miguel knew because he'd seen the dudes she brought to work events. Guys like Phillip from her phone call yesterday.

If Miguel was feeling possessive, it was only because he needed her focused to keep his job. He didn't need some blond corporate asshole taking her mind off their mission. They were here to be the best of the best and nothing was going to stand in his way. What was needed here was a subtle, "Back off, asshole. I see you staring at her" move.

So he palmed her shoulder casually. "I had my first kiss at camp," he said while resisting the urge to tug on her ponytail.

She turned around and craned her neck to see him. Without her heels, she was even tinier than usual. Which was supposed to slow down that punch in his chest when he realized she hadn't covered her freckles with makeup today. "I've never been to camp."

Figures. She didn't muss, after all. That should have been enough to calm him down right?

She turned back around. That wouldn't do. Blond Asshole was still watching. And Miguel didn't like being dismissed. He leaned down, close to her ear, inhaling her scent. Pears. "Her name was Shelly. She was thirteen. I got to second base."

Sera had stiffened while he spoke in her ear, but she couldn't cover up the little shiver. And the little shiver gave him pause. Just a twinge. Nothing really. So she was sensitive near her ear. Who wasn't?

She tilted her chin slightly, but didn't turn her whole body this time. "Why are you telling me this?"

"I figure we should get to know each other better. Part of the team building process, you know? Who was your first kiss?"

"How is that going to help us, exactly?"

He sighed. "We need to be more comfortable with each other. And if you've never been to camp, you've probably never done a three-legged race. If I'm going to be tied to your leg, you need to get to know me better."

Her turn to sigh as they shuffled forward, getting closer to the counselors doing paperwork. Counselors—he'd had a crush on just about all of the teen girls when he went to camp as a kid. Maybe he could fulfill a fantasy or two while they were stuck here.

Summer camp for grownups. It was ingenious really. And he could already see the marketing opportunities as he looked around. All the things a person loved about childhood with the added freedom of being an adult. He was sorry he hadn't thought of the idea himself. He tried to imagine what it would be like to work outside all day instead of being cooped up in an office. Playing volleyball, going canoeing, telling ghost stories around a campfire…it sounded like his idea of a perfect retirement. All the things he loved.

But retirement, the kind he was looking forward to, cost way more than he could make working at a summer camp. So he'd have to deal with a few more years of traffic and people and noise to fund the life he wanted in fifteen years.

Someone came around with red cups of beer to make standing in line a little easier. He wasn't surprised when Sera turned one down. Nor was he surprised when she huffed disdainfully when he gladly took one for himself.

"What?" he asked.

"It's barely noon yet."

"So?"

"So? It's a little early for drinking."

"Are you going to be like this the whole week or do you think you'll mellow out eventually?" The second the words tumbled out of his mouth, he wished he could take them back.

Sera flushed a pretty pink as she bit back the retort he deserved. He really couldn't blame her for getting mad. They were supposed to be getting along, building a team, and he shouldn't have picked on her like that. He hated that she was better at not giving in to a petty argument than he was. But she held it in.

"I'm sorry, Sera."

The eyebrow winged up as she waited for another zinger. When nothing came, she nodded. "I don't mean to be prickly. I'm not always, you know."

"I just bring it out in you, huh?"

She studied him for a moment. She looked more vulnerable without her red lipstick. Without the makeup covering her freckles. "I don't know why you do, but yes. For some reason, I am not my very best self around you."

He wanted to say he wasn't either. He wanted to acknowledge that he appreciated the moment of honesty they were having. He wanted to tug on her ponytail. But then it was their turn to sign in and the moment vanished like the light of a firefly.

They signed the waivers, took their maps, listened to the speech.

"Great!" the sunny blonde said, handing them each a key and pointing to the map on the table. "You're in cabin nine. There is a pre-dinner cocktail reception in the boathouse at five o'clock. Hope to see you there."

"We're in the same cabin?" Sera asked. "Aren't the boys and girls separated? Like …at camp?"

"Usually, yes. But for Rediscover Marital Intimacy sessions, we put the married couples together. It's all about romance." She winked.

"What?" Sera asked and looked at Miguel.

"Did you say Rediscover Marital Intimacy?" His mind wasn't processing. That was—well it didn't sound like any corporate team building he'd ever been to. "There's been a mistake."

"Oh," Blondie said. "They renamed it in February. If you signed up before that, it was called Marriage Booster. But don't worry, it's all the same great stuff. You're going to leave here feeling just as good about life as you did after your honeymoon. We promise. This week will strengthen your marriage

"Our marriage," Sera repeated slowly. Like saying it at a reduced speed would clear up the misunderstanding.

"It's a week-long love fest, I promise. Sometimes it borders on hedonistic. You're gonna feel just a little naughty all week. And, if you're really good, you two could win the grand prize."

Oh shit. Mr. Martin's demands came rippling back through his mind. Certificates, awards…prizes…How does one "win" a grand prize at being married?

Sera started to panic. He could tell because she was losing her icy exterior. Like a snow sculpture with one good crack, the ice princess was losing her cool. And sputtering a little. "There has been a terrible misunderstanding. We can't possibly—"

"Lose," Miguel interrupted her. "We can't possibly lose." He slung an arm around her shoulder and squeezed. "Sweetheart, we are going to mop up the competition. The grand prize is in the bag."

"The grand prize…" She paled. "One…two…three…" she replied.

Okay then. His wife was no longer coherent. It was up to Miguel to get this circus back under the big top. He gathered their bags and moved her in the direction of the cabins.

"Six…seven…eight."

"That's it, dear."

Luckily, she'd packed light. Efficient as always, he supposed. She counted to ten again and he didn't try to interrupt. His mind was racing too. He'd expected corporate types doing team building exercises forced on them by upper management. Maybe some role playing. He hadn't expected to have to play the part of a husband.

Ever.

"Do you think Mr. Martin made a mistake or is he really this evil?" She'd managed to pull herself together in time to unlock the door since his arms were full.

He really needed to set this stuff…down. He looked around a blew out a long whistle before dropping the bags.

The cabin decor was rustic, yet he noted the a/c unit in the window. But it wasn't the log walls or plaid curtains that kept his attention. It was the bed.

The not very big bed in the center of the room. The bed covered in rose petals. Four Mylar heart balloons were tied to the posts. And a bucket of ice was chilling a bottle on the bedside table.

"Wow."

"Agreed," he said.

She barked out a single, harsh laugh. "See, Mr. Castillo? It's already working."

THE WALLS SEEMED TO SHRINK THE longer Sera looked at that bed in the middle of the room.

"I don't understand how this happened," she said aloud, though not directly to Miguel because he couldn't help. They were stuck. For a whole week. "Should we call Mr. Martin? Tell him he signed us up for the wrong session?"

He lowered into one of the two chairs in the cabin. "I'm not sure that's a good idea. He was pretty adamant that we find a way to handle things. I think we should show him we can."

"They think we're married."

"I realize that."

She took the other chair across the tiny table and started to look over their itinerary. Sunrise couples yoga. Ballroom dancing. Canoe trips. "Marriage counseling!"

"What?" He took the paper from her hands. "We have to go to marriage counseling?"

"I think we need to tell the staff there has been a mistake. We'll never make it through marriage counseling without them figuring it out anyway."

"Sure we can. We'll just pretend to be completely happy together. They'll realize we don't need counseling. Maybe we can win 'Most in love' or something. Martin told us to come back with every award they offered. That counselor mentioned a grand prize."

She took the agenda back. "I'm pretty sure they don't offer prizes in therapy. If we are going to do this, we need to figure out our cover story."

He smiled. Oh God, she'd forgotten he had dimples. Laugh lines and dimples should be outlawed. It was a potent combination. "I like the way you think, princess."

"Don't call me that."

He grinned. Dammit she almost smiled back.

"So what's our story?" he asked. "We're going to need a backstory for this campaign."

Campaign. They were the two best shining stars at a respectable advertising agency. They could sell anything to anyone. That's all this was. They were marketing themselves. This they could do. She pulled a notebook and pen from her bag. "We've been married for…two years?"

"Okay. Why are we here? I don't want anyone thinking we've already lost our intimacy after two years of marriage."

Figures. That's just like a man to not be able to accept he needs help for something. "Fine. We are here because …" She looked over some of the material in the folder. "…of the fireflies."

"Fireflies?"

"Yes. I really like fireflies and this brochure talks about how people come from all over to see them. We thought it would be romantic. We've both been working too hard." She actually wasn't sure she liked fireflies at all. They were insects. She didn't have much experience with insects, but she knew she didn't care for them.

Miguel drummed his fingers on the small tabletop, a habit she knew meant he was getting on a roll. "We needed to get away from wi-fi and our jobs and just get back to nature."

"Okay. Great. So, we have the perfect marriage. Totally in love. We're just here for downtime and bugs that light up."

"When did we meet?" he asked, but his eyes kept drifting to the bed.

"Let's just keep it simple. When did we meet for real? Four years ago?"

He nodded. "Okay. Yeah. We met at work. We're both in advertising."

"Where did we get married?" She kept her own eyes trained on him and not the elephant draped in plaid in the center of the room.

"Saint Mary's in my hometown of—"

"I don't think so."

His brows knit together. What's wrong with Saint Mary's?"

Honestly. "Miguel, I'm Jewish. We can't get married in a Catholic church."

He was genuinely surprised. "My family is going to flip out unless you convert."

"I'm not converting. You convert."

Tension stretched between them. "How about we have a nondenominational wedding?"

"Agreed."

They both smiled at the implied, *See, it's already working.*

He sat back in the chair. That slouch that annoyed her so much in the city was actually not so bad in the cabin. "How are we going to raise our kids then? If neither of us converts."

She couldn't help but smile at the thought of Miguel dripping with small children. "As little agnostic heathens?"

"Agreed. Okay. Where did we get married? Honeymoon? We should pick someplace we've both been."

They worked out more details of their faux perfect relationship until it became almost fun.

"I will concede to the Prius," he said, "but we have a dog not a cat."

"Can we have both?" she asked, her heart aching a little for her fluffy gray cat at home. Cobain was worth the extra time she had to spend with a lint roller several times a day, and she'd hated leaving him with her mother for the week. Mom wasn't exactly responsible. Exhibit A: Sera who'd had to practically get a medical degree at the age of eight because her mother forgot things when she was into her art and/or off her meds. Exhibit B: The back payments Sera was currently making on her mom's house because she'd forgotten to pay for months.

But Cobain was pretty low maintenance, and Sera had hidden little bowls of food and water all over the house in case Mom forgot. He also wasn't shy about yowling when he wanted something, so she had to believe he'd be fine for a week.

"A cat, huh?" Miguel grimaced at her until she schooled her expression. "If it means that much to you, we can have a cat and a dog, dear. Who's taking care of them while we're gone. I hope Fido isn't peeing on that carpet we just installed in the office."

"You act like you did it yourself."

"Oh, I did. And you helped me. Weekend warrior project."

She smiled at the thought of them installing carpet together. They hadn't been able to order lunch together successfully last week. "I hadn't realized you were so handy."

"It took a lot longer than we thought it would because…well, you on your hands and knees all day. It was distracting."

She felt her blush and kicked him under the table. "Go make me a sandwich, Castillo."

When he laughed out loud, something bloomed inside her chest like pride. And she was going to have to squash that. No chest bloomings. Her heart had survived two surgeries and a lifetime of meds, but she wasn't about to subject it to the likes of a man like Miguel.

"Are we ready for the cocktail reception? Because I am more than ready for a drink."

She nodded, grateful that the entire week was unlimited booze. "I'd like to unpack first. But I can meet you there."

"Oh no, our first appearance as man and wife is important. I'll wait."

"Are you going to unpack?"

"Nah."

She'd seen movies about camp and realized that Camp Firefly Falls was a step above. For one thing, they had their own bathroom. No outhouses or midnight trips through the woods with a flashlight. For another, well, the bed. It just sat there in the middle of the room. All made up and waiting where she'd expected to find wooden bunks and sleeping bags. The floor looked hard and uninviting, and she imagined it would be a cold day in hell before she convinced Miguel to sleep on it. No, they'd have to share the bed. They were both adults. They could do this.

After a couple of cocktails she could, anyway.

The boathouse was done up with a canopy of white lights. It was charming and romantic and holding hands with her husband while she threw back a G&T was surreal. Since they didn't know what the grand prize was or what the judging requirements for winning it would be, they were not sure if they were already in some sort of competition. If there really was a "Most in Love" they were planning on winning.

He leaned down and placed a soft kiss on her temple while whispering, "Okay, if we are in the same room, we are always touching. Got it?"

As if he knew more about being in a committed relationship than she did.

Which admittedly wasn't a lot. But she'd at least brought the same man to more than one company function while Miguel had a new date every time.

It was his wandering eye they needed to be concerned about. She cupped his cheek. "You are a man in love. If I am anywhere near you, your eyes will seek me out. You will stop checking out the counselors and the other *married* women in the room. You have eyes only for your beloved wife."

He chuckled softly. "Of course, dear. Besides, the way you will always be touching me, kissing me, my eyes won't have time to stray will they?"

The thought of touching him constantly for the next week wasn't as daunting as it should have been. She made it a practice to never lie to herself, so she had to admit she was actually looking forward to this play-acting. Which was so wrong. But as long as she remembered it was a ruse, it couldn't hurt her. In fact, they were hurting no one. It was a game.

So she kissed him.

The surprised "oh" of his mouth softened and he kissed her back, slowly, softly, until she realized the soft moan she heard had been her own. She pulled back, amazed to see his dark eyes almost black from his dilated pupils. You can't fake dilated pupils. Hers probably looked the same and she realized she was in deep trouble.

"Get a room," a voice interrupted.

"Shut up, Steve." The man, not Steve, held out a hand. "I apologize. My husband thinks he's funny. I'm Neil."

After shaking hands with Neil, Miguel's arm went around her waist like it was the most natural thing in the world.

Neil and Steve owned a small hobby farm in which Steve farmed the sheep and Neil spun the wool and sold hand-knit hats on Etsy.

"We're having a baby in three months, so we thought we'd do one last couple-focused vacation. This wasn't my first choice," Neil said, gesturing to Steve. "He likes zip-lining and I like not zip-lining, but we really wanted to be around people with like minds about their marriages. You guys have kids?"

"No," Miguel answered quickly. Too quickly. "We're not ready."

"I like knitting," Sera said to cover his obvious discomfort. "It's very relaxing."

"Did you bring your needles?" When she shook her head, Neil said, "I brought extra. You can try some of our wool. You'll never go back to store bought again."

Steve and Miguel made plans to sign up for zip-lining and jet skis. Neil and Sera made plans for reading books while drunk. Another couple, Layla and Brad, introduced themselves and all six of them sat together at dinner. At the campfire after dinner, everyone at camp came down and then began drinking in earnest. It was tempting to do the same, but she'd had such a long day already, and sunrise yoga looming over her head, she begged off.

Her husband wouldn't take no for an answer when it came time to walk back to the cabin.

"You don't have to come with me. You were enjoying yourself."

"I'm not letting my wife walk alone in the woods. Besides, it wouldn't look right if I passed up an opportunity to get you alone in the cabin on a week devoted to boosting our intimacy, would it?"

She felt herself growing colder. Not because he was wrong, but because it was too easy to pretend. She liked it when he called her his wife. She knew she was lonely, but she hadn't realized just how alone she felt until she warmed so quickly to the thought of someone caring about her walking alone in the woods.

She had to shut this down. Now was not the time to think about that kiss or the warm, gooey feelings she got when he pretended to be in love with her all night.

When he opened the cabin door and she stepped inside, she could practically hear the sound of the record scratching as all sound in her head came to a complete halt.

That damned bed.

"How are we going to do this?" she asked him, hoping beyond hope he would stay true to his gentlemanly manners and offer to sleep on the floor.

"We go to sleep," he answered instead.

"Right."

He lifted his shirt in one swift motion. "Afraid you can't control yourself, honey?"

"Oh, I'm not worried about me." But she was. She so was.

He was amazing. His muscles were chiseled by the finest sculptor ever, and the lines of his frame tapered in a way that made her hands itch to trace the line. They worked in advertising, for crying out loud. Where did he come up with a body like that?

But no way she let him get the upper hand here. She released her pony tail like it was the Kraken. Shaking out her hair bad shampoo-commercial style, she unbuttoned the oversized flannel she'd thrown over a tank top before dinner.

He didn't even try to mask his interest. "Whose shirt is that?" he asked.

"Mine."

"Who did it used to belong to?" His voice...well, it cracked. "It's a man's shirt. I can tell by the buttons."

She paused unbuttoning it. "Does it matter?" Did he care? Was he jealous?

"It does if he's still in the picture. Since I'll be sleeping with his girlfriend tonight."

Their gazes locked and held for several long seconds that felt like hours. Finally, she shook her head. "There's no one. I'm not seeing anyone right now." She'd been giving Phillip the heave-ho when Miguel had interrupted her phone call yesterday.

"Me either." Which she assumed, but she probably should have asked before she'd kissed him.

So. They had gone from barely tolerating each other, to pretending to be married, kissing, and now getting into bed together after establishing they were both single. This day could not have turned out more differently than she'd expected.

His eyes were hungry, but she couldn't stop poking the bear as she slid the shirt off her shoulders. He took two steps toward her but paused and reached past her, grabbing his shave kit from the bureau behind her. Her chest was inches from grazing his. She was within kissing distance of the pulse point on his neck that beat faster because of her. "Mind if I take the bathroom first?" he asked.

She couldn't translate the words very fast. Like he was speaking Swahili instead of English. She was afraid she was alone in the sea of rising lust, but one glance down his lower body spoke of his desire matching hers. She traveled the line back up the happy trail until she met his gaze. And his smirk.

Jerk.

"No, you should definitely go first. You have some things to …take care of," she said pointedly, sending him a matching smirk.

He wasn't in the bathroom but five minutes, and her pulse still raced while she took her turn. She hoped she took long enough in the bathroom that he would be asleep when she got into bed. Whether he was or not, slipping into the soft clean sheets had been heavenly, and she drifted off as soon as her head hit the pillow.

Tomorrow could take care of itself. She'd had all she could be reasonably expected to take for today.

CHAPTER THREE

> **Good morning, Campers!**
> Hopefully you didn't have too much fun at the mixer and campfire last night and are ready for some hot, summer fun. If you did overindulge, go back to the scene of the crime where we've stashed blue coolers filled with Heather Tully's Secret Hangover Remedy (pour yourself a glass from the pitcher) If hair of the dog is more your style, the red coolers are stocked with cans of beer and tomato juice.
>
> If you've never tried couples' yoga, you don't know what you've been missing. We know it's early, but you won't regret greeting the day with your beloved and learning some sexy, intimate poses.
>
>
> **Day Two for Sera and Miguel**
> Sunrise Yoga: 7:30 a.m.
> Softball practice: 9 a.m.
> Marriage Counseling: 1 p.m.

MIGUEL HAD NEVER EATEN SMOKED pears before, but as he woke up by degrees, he realized he'd been dreaming about them.

And then he figured out why.

Sera's hair, which usually smelled like pears, had absorbed some campfire smoke the night before, and her hair was under his nose. And his body was curved around hers like spoons in a drawer. Which meant if she woke up now, she would feel just how much he was enjoying waking up wrapped around her. Because she felt really good pressed up against him.

Really good.

It wasn't often that he woke up wrapped around a woman. He wasn't a spend the night kind of guy. It sent an impression he wasn't interested in maintaining. He wasn't a manwhore, either. It's not like he was out getting laid every weekend with random one night stands. But on the nights when he wasn't being a monk, he did not usually fall asleep with a woman.

Sera mumbled something, and he couldn't resist pulling her in a little tighter.

He told himself that the sexual tension between them was a good thing. It would make their charade more believable. It would make it easier to look like they were in love if they looked like they wanted to bang each other. He told himself that holding her close right now would help make touching her later seem more natural.

He could tell himself whatever he wanted. The simple truth was that it didn't matter if she wasn't wearing the pencil skirt or that her hair smelled like smoke or that she annoyed him by simply existing. He was spooning Sera Worth because there was nothing on earth he'd rather do at that moment than hold her close and smell her, smoke and all.

Okay, there was something else he wanted to do.

But sex was off the table. They still had to go back to the real world after this one-week marriage fantasy. Sex would complicate things way too much.

He let himself drift back to sleep until she started shifting around in his arms. He cracked open one eye to find her staring at him over her shoulder.

"Good morning, husband." Her voice was crackly. He guessed he assumed she woke up just as smooth and polished as she showed up to the office. Her hair was everywhere...she definitely did muss after all. Because she looked and sounded like the kind of woman you drag back into bed when she tried to get out.

"Morning, wife."

She rolled until she was facing him all the way, but there wasn't a lot of room on the bed, and she didn't strive to put more space between them. "Did you sleep well?"

"Like a rock." Her eyes were so big. Had her eyes always been like that? So expressive? He didn't know her well enough to pick up what she was feeling, but in a weird way, he wished he did.

"I was thinking about the sheep farm."

Huh? "Huh?"

"Well, I know that they make a little bit of money selling the raw wool and the hats that Neil makes and sells on Etsy. But I'm wondering if they could do farm tours. Maybe even a small scale B&B. And Neil could have a physical shop where he does his knitting during the day where people can come in and buy yarn. He has to knit somewhere; it might as well be someplace where he could sell his wares at the same time."

"That's what you were thinking about this morning?"

She nodded, and sure enough, her eyes had a little light behind them. Like the spark from her thought was lighting them up and he could see her thinking.

"That's not what I was thinking about," he admitted. Though it was a good idea. Hobby farms were on trend right now.

She giggled softly. "I know. I felt you thinking against my ass."

He'd never heard her giggle before. And he'd never heard her swear. This trip was getting better all the time because he was going to make it his mission to hear them both more often. "Does it bother you?"

"That you woke up with an erection? No. That's kind of what guys do."

"You're not going to try and take any credit for it? I think you should."

There was something very soothing about the intimacy of their morning talk. Yeah, he wanted to bone her, but the soft light and hushed voices and cocoon of blankets wasn't encouraging him to jump out of bed and start the day. Nobody could see them in the cabin. It wasn't about fooling everyone into thinking they were a couple. It was just the two of them without the office or the competition or the expectations of anyone else.

But all good things must end and they made their way to sunrise yoga on the waterfront. Pre-coffee.

This probably wasn't going to end well.

Lake Waawaatesi was calm and beautiful. A good day for paddle boarding. If nothing else, this trip was worth it for the scenery. Just breathing out here felt better.

The dock was large, but it would have to be to accommodate all the yoga enthusiasts. Not everyone was up at dawn for the session—but he and Sera had decided to be everywhere they could in case they were being judged. Sleeping in would have been nice, but the peace of a day not yet begun was nice too.

They took two mats and settled in, watching as two extremely fit people got in position. A man and a woman.

"Good morning everyone. My name is Essa and this is Birk. We're going to spend every dawn with you for the next week."

Birk? Seriously? Did yoga instructors take on stage names? The guy was a piece of work. More muscle than brain. Or maybe Miguel was just jealous.

Nah. He hated Birk on sight.

"Yoga for couples is extremely beneficial for creating bonds and strengthening intimacy. We'll start with very beginner and basic poses, but by the end of our time together, you'll have a couple of tantric poses in your repertoire as well."

He'd heard the word tantric before, so he glanced at his partner who looked alarmed.

"Doing yoga together will build trust and unity. You will find that if you give into the breathing, you and your partner will unite in similar rhythms. Your breathing and heartbeats will synchronize and you'll feel in tune with each other in ways you never imagined before. The trust comes as you learn each other's limitations, as you rely on each other to stretch and extend out of yourself."

He looked around and was relieved to see other people were nervous. Except Steve and Neil. Maybe they did yoga together already.

"We'll begin by sitting cross-legged and knee to knee, so if you'll face each other on the mats, we'll start."

As they sat, he noticed how easily Sera moved her legs into position. She was already bendy where he was not.

"Okay now, Birk and I are going to show you the "heart hug" by putting our left hands over each other's hearts and our right hands in Namaste prayer position." They got onto their mats and asked everyone to copy their pose. "Now close your eyes and breathe. Just relax and allow your breathing to synchronize."

After a few minutes of breathing, they were taught three more poses and it was all…nice. Until they did something called "child's pose with upward dog."

Brick and Essa showed the pose first, and he got hot. Very hot. All over. It was basically doggy style with clothes. Now that he and Sera were so "in sync" with each other, they mentally communicated that he be the first into child's position. But when the direction from Essa came, "lean your hips forward into the upward dog while resting your hips on your partner's sacrum," he was sure he was going to flip Sera over and maul her in front of everyone. When they switched, he didn't even care about it being awkward anymore. He wanted to rest on her sacrum more than he'd wanted anything in a very long time.

She felt good. Better than good.

"Miguel?" she asked as they held the pose.

"Yes, Sera?"

She didn't answer. They just kept breathing and neither the question nor the answer felt all that important anyway. He concentrated on the sound of the water lapping against the dock supports below them, the sky gentling from pink to blue, the cry of fishing birds on the lake, and the smell of pears and the rich scent of the wood surrounding them. He hadn't ever felt so present in a moment. He'd deny it if anyone asked, but he could feel her heart beating inside of him. A small vibration pulling at him.

After yoga, after a cold shower, after breakfast, and after another cold shower, they had softball.

"I can't do this," Sera said, the panicked look in her eye concerning him.

"Why?" he pulled her away from the line. Today and tomorrow they practiced. Then the intramural games would start for the week.

He didn't like her color and found he could name another of her moods based on her expressive eyes. Terror.

"I'm not good at sports."

It was more than that, but he didn't want to push her. "I saw you contort your body into several poses this morning. You're strong, toned, and flexible. What's really wrong."

"I don't know how to play. I've never…I've never even held a bat."

What kind of childhood included never holding a bat?

He didn't care if they lost every game they played, Mr. Martin be damned, but he was going to erase that look of terror from her eyes.

"Hey, princess. We got this." Once more, he was spooned around her body, but this time he was molding her hands around the bat, one palm up, one down.

"I'm not very strong," she protested.

"You don't need to be." He slid his hands to her hips. "This is where your power is."

She twisted her head to give him a sidelong glance. "My hips?"

"Yep. And here." He tapped her head. "'Hitting is fifty percent above the shoulders.' That's a quote from Ted Williams."

"Who is Ted Williams?"

"Later." He walked her through a couple swings, blaming the warming day for the heat even while knowing it came from inside him. He needed to stop touching her, but he couldn't. He was a pig. The worst kind.

"We have free time after this until lunch. I could use a swim," she said, as if the image he conjured of her in a swimsuit was no big deal.

Maybe the cold water would be good for him. He definitely needed a cool down.

SERA WORRIED THAT THE BEER might have been a bad idea right before seeing a marriage counselor, but she drank it anyway. Beer had never tasted so good as they relaxed in the Adirondack lounge chairs overlooking the lake and made their story airtight.

"We really do have a great marriage, Miguel."

He laughed. "You don't think the Eiffel Tower proposal was too much?"

"Maybe a little. I think I'd rather be proposed to in private."

He considered her carefully for a moment, his head cocked to one side. "A sensible proposal, right? Hell, you probably didn't even want me to ask. You would prefer a quiet discussion of the reasons to get married versus staying single."

"Well, yes. Marriage shouldn't be a yes or no question asked by the man."

Miguel held his hand up. "I get it. You've never been in love."

One. Two. Three…

"I can see you counting," he said. The teasing lilt in his voice just made her more agitated. "You count a lot."

"I certainly do," she answered and swigged down the last third of her beer. "What makes you think I've never been in love? Just because I'm practical doesn't mean I can't also have feelings."

"I don't doubt your capability of having feelings, princess. I'm just saying you've never been swept away by them. A marriage proposal isn't supposed to be practical."

"I see. And you know this because you've proposed so many times then?"

A flare lit his eyes from behind and then poofed out just as quickly. "Just once."

His answer staggered her, but he was closing down and she wasn't going to get more out of him than that. He checked his watch and stood.

"Miguel…"

"It's time to go to counseling. I proposed to you in Paris. I swept you off your feet." He held out his hand to help her out of her chair. "You can be practical about a lot of things, Sera, but being in love with me isn't one of them."

A cold flush swept over her body at his words. That would be the problem with a guy like Miguel. A woman can forget herself, lose herself, when she's in love. Sera couldn't allow herself that kind of chaos.

They met their counselor, who turned out to be Birk from yoga, in an office with several of his diplomas on the wall. The office overlooked the lake from the second floor of the lodge. The lodge itself was going to be pretty grand, but it was still undergoing rehab construction.

Birk was handsome. Under other circumstances, she'd have probably dated him. She self-consciously rubbed the ring on her left hand—she'd transferred the band she usually wore from her right. Her movement drew Birk's eyes and she worried. Was that some kind of signal to a therapist? Marriage in trouble?

She and Miguel sat next to each other on the couch and Birk took a chair across from them. "How did you enjoy yoga this morning?" he began.

She felt the fire of the blush to her toes. "It was relaxing." *It was the hottest thing I've ever done fully clothed.* "The lake is beautiful."

Her husband chuckled. "I'm not sure relaxing is the right word. I needed two cold showers this morning. If they want us to discover our intimacy, they might need to leave us more free time on the agenda."

Birk raised a brow. "Rediscover."

"Huh?" Miguel asked.

"It's rediscover intimacy. And intimacy is more than sex."

Miguel appraised Birk for a long moment. "We're not here to fix a troubled marriage. My wife and I don't need to 'rediscover' anything. Camp sounded fun. She likes fireflies. I like zip-lining. And our intimacy is just fine, thank you."

Birk sat back in his chair. "I didn't mean to offend."

"I'm not offended."

He was just being super defensive. What was up with him? She laid her hand on his knee and he immediately covered it with his own. "We've never had a counseling session. We're not sure what to expect."

Birk nodded. "This hour—"

"Fifty minutes," Miguel interjected.

"Huh?"

Miguel squeezed her hand. "That's how counseling works, right? You call it an hour, but it's really fifty minutes."

Birk didn't look old enough to be a counselor. He didn't look like he spent an hour away from the gym on any given day, and yeah, she was objectifying him based on his looks, but he didn't look like he could handle a battle of wits with a guy like Miguel. But instead of rising to Miguel's bait, he simply answered, "Fifty minutes."

Miguel tensed up. What was his beef with Birk?

Birk continued, "This is really your time. We can tackle a problem or we can strengthen bonds. Communication is often where most couples choose to utilize their sessions. But I'm trained in several disciplines, so we can tailor this to you."

"Well, we don't really have anything to work out. Things are going great. Right, princess?"

Gah. She hated that name. "Never been better," she said tightly.

Birk eyed them coolly. "That's great," he said finally. He cocked his head and scrutinized Miguel for a moment. "You'll love the zip-line."

"I'm looking forward to it," Miguel answered. Did he know he was stroking her hand? The pattern was soothing despite the fact that she had a feeling Birk wasn't buying their happy marriage charade.

"And you, Sera? Are you looking forward to zip-lining?"

"Ah, no. I'll be reading a book in one of those nice chairs while he's off adventuring."

Birk rubbed his chin and considered her. "And why is that?"

"I don't like high adrenaline sports. I leave that to Miguel."

"And how does that make you feel, Miguel? That your wife doesn't share the same love of sports you do?"

"It's fine."

"Do you wish she'd join you?"

"Only if she wants to."

"It must make you feel lonely sometimes," he said to Sera. "When Miguel goes off and leaves you alone."

Well, now she felt defensive. "My husband and I are adults with varied interests. It's more than fine with me that he enjoys himself."

"Do you two have any mutual interests?"

"Look," Miguel began. "I like zip-lining, but I love my wife. We work together sixty hours a week, so we occasionally do our own thing. But," he squeezed her hand and met her eyes with his, "nothing beats coming home. The sports are fun, but nothing compares to knowing she's got my back and I've got hers. I love going home, man. Sera is my whole world."

She'd underestimated his marketing skills. She'd known he was good, but she hadn't known that Miguel could make her believe, even for an instant, that what he wanted was marriage, a home…her. She could feel that new carpet under her feet in the den, taste the wine they sipped in front of the fireplace on cold winter evenings, and she knew the weight of his body when they made love in the bed they shared in the city. The real world slipped away and she slipped into the alternate universe he created.

She was greedy with the want of it.

"Is our fifty up, Birk?" he asked, not losing eye contact. "My wife and I have…things to do."

Oh my. She needed a guardrail and fast or she was going to careen right into the abyss. Everything went liquid inside her.

Guys like Miguel were candy. He had nothing to offer her but empty calories. But she'd dieted for so long, hadn't she? Sensible meals planned, nutritional values met, and careful ratios considered—she could afford to indulge in something sinful once in a while, couldn't she?

No. No she could not.

Sera looked away and broke the spell. "I think we should give Birk a chance. We paid for this, after all."

Miguel closed off then. Disappointed? Maybe. But it was for the best.

CHAPTER FOUR

> **Good morning, Campers!**
>
> We hope you'll join us for a picnic lunch on the greenfield today. We're featuring a live band from the neighboring town of Briarsted.
>
> We've also got only two more openings for couples massages today—stop by the lodge to make your reservation. After dinner tonight is Capture the Flag, so you might want to get a nap in after lunch.
>
> **Day Three**
> Sunrise Yoga: 7:30 a.m.
> Softball practice: 9 a.m. to 10 a.m.
> Arts and Crafts: 10:15 a.m.-11:15 a.m.
> Counseling session: 1 p.m.

MIGUEL HELD THE DOOR FOR Sera as they entered the arts and crafts cabin. It smelled like clay and wood shavings, much like his memories of crafts from summers long gone. He'd learned to whittle and braid friendship bracelets when he was a kid. There was probably more, but that was all he could recall.

Sera took seats across the table from Steve and Neil. They'd sat together at dinner last night too. The couple had great stories about their first few years settling their homestead. Funny stories mostly, but Miguel knew it couldn't have been easy to transition from city living to a farm. Their relationship didn't seem any worse for the wear, and it made him wonder about marriage in general.

As a casual observer, he noticed most relationships strengthened in adversity or failed spectacularly at the smallest bump in the road. He didn't know how you knew which it would be. He figured most people who got married believed they could weather those storms—so what was it that made them unable to?

It's not like it mattered. He wasn't planning on a real wedding at any point, so he'd leave that to the experts like Birk. Jesus. Just thinking of the guy pissed him off.

Sera pulled her attention away from Neil and leaned over to rub Miguel's jaw. "You okay, honey? You're doing that thing you do when you're pissed off."

"What thing?"

She continued to massage from his temple to his chin. "Your jaw gets super square and there's a tic in it."

Huh. He had no idea he had such a tell, but if anyone had the chance to see him get tense, it was Sera.

He grasped her wrist and kissed the inside of it. "I'm fine." Her eyes dilated at the slight press of his lips. He wished they were back in their cabin, cocooned in their nest, and he was kissing more than her wrist.

Miguel had to admit he liked being married on a temporary basis. If you'd told him a week ago that Sera would be an excellent wife for him, he'd have strained a muscle laughing. But it was nice having her on his side for a change—and being on hers. Aside from the fact that she turned him on and pears were suddenly the sexiest scent he could name, he enjoyed her company now. She made him feel grounded—but not bored. But it was more than that. They were a team.

When she had her first solid hit this morning at practice, he hadn't been able to contain himself. He felt the joy break out of him as he swooped her into his arms and twirled her around. It was just a hit—barely made it past the infield, but her success felt better than his own.

And he was still staring into her eyes.

Shit. He had to get a grip. Being attracted to her was one thing. Being infatuated another.

Luckily, a counselor came by and plunked down a cardboard box in the middle of their table, providing a good distraction. A woman named Heather, the owner of the camp, stood at the front of the room and told them to take everything out of the box. There were two sets of knitting needles, a small pie plate, a tea light burner, and four colors of licorice laces.

According to Heather, they were going to knit edible underwear today.

Summer camp was going to kill him.

"Um." Sera bit her lip and the prettiest pink blush painted over her cheeks. "Okay?"

Steve's face was as red as the licorice. "Right. So—since Neil and Sera know how to knit, that puts us on 'yarn' duty then, eh?"

Miguel nodded and they got to work lighting the candle and getting their burner set up. They had to fuse the ends of the licorice together to make one long strand for ease of knitting. He didn't know what that meant, exactly, but Sera and Neil were reading the pattern and seemed to understand what cast on and knit together meant, so Heather and the other counselor spent their time helping the non-knitters and left their table alone.

As Miguel watched Sera and Neil giggle and try to figure how many stitches to cast on for Steve, who apparently was going to be the wearer of Neil's knitted masterpiece, that spot in his chest ached again. Not a bad ache. He just…liked watching her giggle.

The idea of candy panties on Sera was simultaneously absurd and so fucking hot. He doubted she'd wear them—he'd read enough sex articles in *Men's Health* to know sugar was not a good idea near that region of anyone's body. But that didn't stop the fantasy reel in his head. Nibbling the licorice until he made his way to the real sweetness—yeah. He was about done here.

He excused himself and went out to get some air. Five minutes later, Sera joined him at the picnic table, standing in front of him on the bench, the sugared underwear hooked around her finger. "Hello, Mr. Sera."

Miguel chuckled. "Hello, Mrs. Miguel. What have you got there?"

She sent him a smile. A new smile. One he hadn't seen before. It was mysterious and made him want to know all her secrets. One at a time as he learned them all night long. "Just a little candy."

Every ounce of blood in his body headed south, leaving him lightheaded. Christ, he wanted to eat that candy off her body more than he could recall wanting anything in his life. "You gonna share?"

"I don't know if you want any," she transferred the rainbow colored scrap to her other hand and licked the finger she'd brought it out on, "it's awfully sticky."

He tugged her hips so she stood between his legs, enjoying the surprised gasp from her. "Keep it up, Sera. I like it when you use your feminine wiles on me."

"I have no idea what you're talking about."

He hadn't made a conscious decision to kiss her. He hadn't realized he'd started until her mouth opened under his and he had his tongue in her mouth. One second she was talking and the next he was tasting.

He palmed her ass, pulling her closer, but not close enough. He wanted inside her. He didn't care about edible thongs or the fact that they were in the middle of a field in broad daylight. He took one hand from her butt and moved it so he could angle her head. Because deeper. He needed to be deeper.

Sera moaned and it jacked his heart rate even more. He could kiss her forever and not have enough of her.

In the distance, he heard snickers and cheering. And then they both seemed to realize that "distance" wasn't really that far away. Everyone coming out of Arts and Crafts stopped to tease. He pulled back, took one look at her kiss swollen lips and dove back in until she pushed his chest gently.

"You're going to tell me to stop, aren't you?" He groaned and rested his forehead on hers. "Do I need to apologize?"

"Are you sorry you kissed me?"

"Hell no."

"I like kissing you, Miguel."

"I hear a 'but' coming."

Her lips pressed into the familiar line. Sera, wearer of pencil skirts and follower of rules, was back. "But we have to figure out a way to work together when we get home. Getting caught up in a summer camp fling is only going to make things harder next week."

He hated that she was right. "I'm not going to lie—I want you. It's not going to be easy sleeping next to you, doing yoga, pretending we're in love. But you're right. Sex is only going to complicate work."

"So we agree then? We don't cross the line?"

"I didn't say that." Maybe she didn't realize he still had his hands on her ass. "We agree that sex will complicate our jobs. That doesn't mean we aren't going to have it."

He loved the surprise that transformed her features from solemn to confused. He'd been wrong about how to handle her all this time. Keeping her off balance was much better than keeping her pissed off.

"Miguel, we can't."

"Sera, we can't stop ourselves."

Ah, there goes the chin. "Well maybe you don't have any control over your hormones, but I—"

He cut her off with a quick kiss and a pat on the butt before he released her. "You want me just as much as I want you. Now it's only a matter of who breaks first."

She narrowed her eyes. "I have a lot of willpower. I've been honing it a very long time."

"We'll see, princess."

CHAPTER FIVE

> **Good morning, Campers!**
>
> Softball games start today. Let's cheer our teams on.
>
> If you get your kicks above the waistline…then you'll be excited about the chess tournament starting in the library in the main lodge today at nine. (If you're not as excited as we are, it's because you don't know that we serve a special drink that you can only get during Chess. It's called Absolut Pin.) It might not be one night in Bangkok, but the cerebrals and the vodka fans will have a good time today.
>
> As a reminder, skinny dipping is against camp rules. If we catch you, we steal your clothes and hang them on the flag post. You'll notice a pair of boxers up there this morning.
>
> **Day Four**
> Sunrise Yoga: 7:30 a.m.
> Softball game: 10 a.m.-11 a.m.
> Counseling session: 1 p.m.-~~2 p.m.~~ 1:50
> Ballroom Dancing: 3 p.m-4 p.m.

SERA WISHED SHE WERE BACK in the beer garden. Or even their counseling session where they'd told Birk about their wedding two years ago. Their made-up never going to happen wedding that would have made a good commercial for their insurance company account now that she thought about it.

But she didn't want to be here.

Ballroom dancing was something she'd never enjoyed and she imagined Miguel felt about the same about it as she did. He'd probably never even danced before.

She tugged his arm. "They told us we don't have to participate in anything we don't want to. Why don't we skip the dancing?"

He shook his head. "There might be a prize. We need to participate in everything."

She hated it when he was right. They really needed to bring home something to prove to their boss that they'd accomplished their objective. What she wouldn't give for a three-legged race right now.

She didn't think there was going to be a competition for anything. So far, only softball and chess seemed to be judged, and the emphasis hadn't really been on the score as much as cheering each other on and having fun.

They'd won their game this morning, though she'd struck out. Luckily, she redeemed herself by catching a pop-over. No, wait. Pop-up. Truthfully, she'd just been protecting her nose. The fact that she'd kept the ball in her glove was just plain luck. But it was a third out or something, so that meant they won.

Or something.

They entered the boathouse where several other couples milled around. She recognized Layla and Brad from the first night, so they joined them for small talk while they waited for the instructor. They were from California, and Layla certainly looked the part of California Girl. She was the kind of girl Sera's *husband* brought to company functions back in the city—tall, blonde, pretty in a natural way. Layla's husband, Brad, was also tall, blond, and pretty in a natural way. From a marketing standpoint, they were perfectly suited for just about any campaign. Who wouldn't want to be like them, look like them?

Sera didn't think she was jealous. Not really. As sick as she'd been as a child, it was really not a surprise that she'd stayed small despite her mother's above average height. There wasn't a lot of energy leftover for growing when she'd needed all her body's resources to keep her heart beating. She was healthy now, and that's what mattered. It wasn't as if being petite was a detriment to dating. But she couldn't stop watching her husband to see if he was watching Layla.

To Miguel's credit, he'd kept his roving eyes in check as far as she could tell. He also hadn't shaved since they'd arrived, and the grizzly look suited him more than she cared to examine.

"You're staring at me," he said. It was the tilt of his head and the whisper of a smile on his lips that let her know he counted it as a win for their little battle.

Which made her think about that kiss.

Which made her blush.

Which made him grin even more. Damn it.

"Are you guys having a good time so far?" Layla asked. Bless her. Now Sera didn't have to make up some lie about why she was staring at her husband's stubble and thinking about edible underwear.

"We are having a wonderful time," Sera answered. Which was not a lie. While softball hadn't been fun, it wasn't horrible either. And waking up next to Miguel every morning was no hardship. It got cold in the cabin at night, and he was a furnace. This morning, she'd let herself pretend, for just a few minutes, that it was real. That it was more than body heat between them.

She was really a sad excuse lately.

As if noticing her mood dip, Miguel rubbed the small of her back absently while he answered Layla. "I thought we'd have a harder time with the no-phone thing, but it's been nice not being tethered to the rest of the world." He kissed the top of Sera's head. "I like not having anything to think about but my bride."

He was laying it on thick—but she liked it. "How about you two?"

"Oh, we love it here," Brad answered. "Especially the skinny dipping. You two been out yet?"

"Not yet."

"Join us tonight," Layla said. "Meet us at eleven."

Sera would have assumed Layla was coming on to Miguel, except that she wasn't talking to Miguel. She was talking to Sera. And smiling like she'd just offered her a stick of gum and not just asked her to get naked with her and her husband.

"Hello everyone!" the dance instructor said from the stage, saving Sera from having to respond to the skinny dipping invitation. "Those of you who have seen *Dirty Dancing* will recognize some of the dance you will learn over the next few days. We'll be doing the Mambo, Johnny Castle-style."

Oh God. Too much cheese.

She shrank inside and looked for the exit.

Miguel rounded in front of her, making himself a barrier to a quick escape, but also a curiously safe buffer from the world. "You okay, Sera?"

"This just isn't my thing. It's silly."

"I thought all women loved *Dirty Dancing*."

"I like the movie. But this feels weird. Forced."

Cheesy.

"What, you didn't have slumber parties and watch it over and over and dream about the bad boy with a heart of gold and doing the lift?"

"What? No." She'd never been to a slumber party. Maybe if she'd been allowed to be a normal kid, this wouldn't feel so weird. But she was out of her depth right now. "Why aren't you more upset about this? And how do you know about the lift?"

He shrugged in answer and then they watched the instructor and another woman show them the first steps.

When it was their turn, Miguel got into position. "We got this."

"Oh really?'

He dropped his hold and smoothed his hands to her hips. "Look at me." As if she had a choice. "I need you to do two things. First, you have to trust me. If this is going to work, you need to let me lead once in a while, okay? This is one of those times. I know it goes against everything you think you stand for, but you have to trust me or it won't work. I don't want to lead all the time. I won't take you somewhere you don't want to go. I won't let you down. But you have to trust me to do it once in a while. Can you?"

Was she that much of a control freak that he thought she couldn't let him lead on the dance floor? Okay, probably she was. "I don't know. What's the other thing?"

"Huh?"

"You said there were two things. I can't promise one without knowing the other first."

He laughed and put them back in starting position, his hands strong and sure. "The other thing is don't step on the one."

She didn't have time to question him further as the instructor counted out the four beats slowly—and not stepping on the "one" was harder than it sounded even after a semester of dance class. After several minutes, the music started and Miguel led her expertly into the routine—even past what they'd been instructed to do. She knew the steps, but how did he? She started to tense up when the other couples moved to the side to make a ring around the dance floor with her smack dab in the middle of it.

She was not in control and people were watching her. It was like her worst nightmare come to life.

"Trust me," he reminded her. His mambo got a little looser, a little more off the cuff and improvised.

Improvising was not her favorite thing. Obviously.

She'd taken only one semester of ballroom dancing her senior year when the other electives she'd wanted were full, but she didn't know exactly what he was doing—only that he was doing it well. What if she couldn't follow? What if…

I won't let you down.

She had to trust him. She had to let go a little or she would humiliate them both.

So she did something outside of her comfort zone.

She relaxed.

Miguel was a natural dancer and he knew it. Normally, his confidence annoyed her. But on the dance floor, with all his attention focused on her, it made her feel…safe of all things. His gaze smoldered, his hips did things Elvis would be proud of, and she realized she was being seduced to the count of four.

And she wanted him to seduce her. Wanted the things he promised when he took the lead. Wanted his attention and his hands and those damn hips. He brought her closer and the dance became less a show and more an embrace. One that should be done in private, but he was staking a claim and she let him.

He danced her all the way to the door and when it closed behind them, they heard the muted claps of the rest of the class they were leaving behind.

Miguel pressed her against the wall, his strong, lean body holding her up where she would have fallen without him. He was staring at her mouth, still focused completely on her.

"Where did you learn to dance like that?" she asked, trying and failing to break the spell.

"My mom teaches dance at a community center. I think she used to teach classes with me still on her hip. There was always dancing at my house."

"You're very good. You actually made me look coordinated."

"Thank you." His hands squeezed her hips, adjusting her off the ground so they were at eye level to each other and she wrapped her legs around his hips. "You're not uncoordinated. You just have a hard time letting go."

She didn't want to let go now, that was for sure. They were still pressed against the wall so tightly a piece of paper couldn't have slid between them. Every hard, lean edge of him pushed into her. He was turned on—as much as she was—and it was empowering to know she'd done that. She had zero control of him she knew, but she hadn't realized she'd enjoy inciting chaos even more.

The throb in her core certainly welcomed the friction of his erection against her shorts and she shifted her hips just a bit to get a better angle.

"You're going to kill me, Sera."

Her world narrowed to him. Just him. His scent surrounded her. His body supported her. His gaze burned her.

"You're no good to me dead, Castillo."

The smile broke across his face, revealing those laugh lines and that dimple. It was beautiful and dangerous, that smile. Though her body was in no danger of falling, thanks to his strong hold, nothing was propping up her heart. Her foolish, unprotected heart started an uncontrolled roll and it was too late. She'd been stupid to forget that her heart was weak. That even minor negligence on her part would leave it unprotected and defenseless. She'd spent her life safeguarding the damn thing, shielding it, building its defenses. And it wasn't a missed dose of medicine or high cholesterol or any of the myriad of pollutants she'd strived to control.

It was a smile that would do her in.

Not even twenty-four hours ago, he'd challenged her. Said one of them would break first. She really hadn't thought it would be her.

She licked her lips and he groaned, anticipating the kiss they both knew was coming.

"Heads," someone yelled from far away. And a Frisbee *thunk*ed next to her head against the planks of the boathouse.

And it was enough to remind her that she was asking for trouble. That she deserved to get hit on the head for thinking this was a good idea.

"We should get ready for dinner."

Miguel stepped back from the wall and let her slide down his body slowly. "It's gonna happen, sweetheart."

"It shouldn't."

He kissed the top of her head.

"Agreed."

MIGUEL'S BRIDE COULD NOT ROAST a marshmallow to save her life.

Her control freak tendencies ought to mean perfect, golden brown crusty marshmallows with just the right amount of goo on the inside, and yet all she'd accomplished so far were charred balls of lava.

"What am I doing wrong?" she asked.

Nothing as far as he could tell. But she kept distracting him when he was meant to be mentoring her roasting. Once she asked him to hold her stick while she put up her hair. It should have been no big deal. But she bent at the waist and finger combed all those dark tresses, and all he could think about was how they would feel fanned over his body. Then, of course, his eyes rested on her ass and that's where they had stopped. He'd dropped her marshmallow into the fire without knowing it until she asked for it back.

Tonight, the flannel shirt she wore was his. It was too big on her—the one she brought would have been more practical—but he'd asked her to wear it. He didn't know why. Seeing his clothes on her filled him with a primal need he hadn't known he had. He half expected his knuckles to drag on the ground on the way from their cabin to the fire pit.

"I'm going to grab a beer from the keg. Can I get you anything?" Not because he wanted a beer. What he wanted was a distraction from the distraction of his wife.

"If you see a copy of *Roasting Marshmallows for Dummies*, grab me one."

It was too much. She wasn't supposed to be funny. Or cute. Or completely fuckable wearing his clothes. Not for the first time since coming to camp, he discovered he was kissing Sera before he made a conscious decision to kiss her. Call it instinct. Call it a compulsion. Call it losing the line between reality and the story they'd made up, but he couldn't not kiss her.

Her lips were sweet and a little sticky and he would never eat another marshmallow without thinking of this night. Miguel pulled back and found her a little dazed, her eyes not focusing, and even that sent another zing into his groin. His umussable Sera Worth got googly-eyed when he kissed her. He didn't know he had that kind of sway—but he was glad it wasn't just him stuck in this strange mire of attraction.

"Be back in a few," he said so that he wouldn't say all the crazy things he was thinking.

He was standing in a short line at the keg when he heard his name.

"I thought that was you," the man said, holding out his hand for a handshake. "Michael Tully. We interned together at my father's company one summer."

As soon as he heard the name, Miguel recognized him. "Wow. Now I feel old. How are you, man? What's it been? Fifteen years?"

"Give or take. You having a good time? My wife and I own the camp."

Miguel knew his incredulous face gave him away. Last he'd heard, Tully was running his old man's multi-million-dollar company. "That's a big…"

"Change?" Michael grinned. "Yeah. The corporate world got a little stale. But camp is always fun. Heather and I met here as kids. When it came up for sale, she bought it outright and we've been building it back up. It's really her show."

Ah, yes, Heather from the X-rated Arts and Crafts cabin. He remembered Michael had a girlfriend named Heather when they interned together all those years ago. Looks like they were the sticking kind.

Michael filled him in about camp. If they'd have come next week, Michael would have been leading the corporate training sessions. The camp Miguel's boss thought he'd sent them to. Instead, Miguel had to lie to his friend and point out his wife across the way who'd been commandeered by Layla again. It seemed Layla and Brad were not only their biggest competition this week—their PDAs were more than just a little excessive, but the couple was also everywhere. Every time he looked up, there they were.

He gave Michael an abbreviated version of their *love* story and then Michael got called away by an employee with some sort of karaoke crisis.

It was time to rescue his wife from Layla anyway. They'd already agreed they didn't want to go skinny dipping last night but had decided they needed to be as diplomatic as possible about declining the invitation—which had been issued again for tonight. They still weren't sure what they had to do to win the prize at the end of the week. If it was a popularity vote, they couldn't afford to hurt anyone's feelings—even if it was sort of inappropriate to invite people you barely knew to get naked and go swimming with you.

But alliances were important. If there really was a Best in Show, he kinda thought it belonged to Neil and Steve. But that didn't mean he wasn't trying to win it.

Layla was a toucher after a few drinks, as advertised by the way she was interacting with Sera as he made his way back around the fire. The whole time she talked, she was holding on to Sera's arm or squeezing a shoulder, an elbow—whatever she could reach. When she put her arm around her as he arrived at the log they were sitting on, she sent Miguel a knowing look and licked her lips.

He stepped back like she'd just threatened to shank him and looked for Layla's husband, only to find Brad on the other side of the fire, watching the ladies intently.

Something was...not quite right about the whole situation. Right now, Layla was looking at him like she wanted to devour him whole but touching his bride like she didn't want to leave her out. Paired with Brad standing twenty feet away and staring like a creeper, it was starting to look a lot like summer camp was way more grown up than he remembered it being.

"So, we'll see you in about an hour?" Layla asked Sera as he arrived on scene.

Sera's deer in the headlights expression was all he needed to go into protection mode. And then she started counting. Not out loud, but he could tell she was doing it. He'd seen it enough. "Probably not tonight," Miguel interrupted. "We have plans."

"Shame," Layla said, brushing her hand to Sera's knee. "We'll miss you. Sera, at least come to the bathroom with me. I don't want to go alone."

"Um…okay."

Without words, she communicated to Miguel that she could handle the field trip to the latrine, but she wished she didn't have to. He hoped she saw that he wished he could rescue her. Because he really wanted to. Rescue her. Which was strange since he'd been trying to throw her under a bus for most of the year.

Less than a week ago, he didn't like her. Other than mutual dislike for each other, they hadn't agreed on anything for months. And before the promotion, he might have even said he hated her. And Miguel hadn't hated anyone since Ricky Price told everyone he still wet the bed in second grade.

So, yeah, he and Sera hadn't been much better than second graders.

But he didn't hate her anymore. If he didn't know any better, he'd have to say he liked her.

It was the circumstances though, right? They were thrown together in a strange land with a shared goal: to make it out alive. Forced proximity created the appearance of a relationship.

But that didn't feel right. Maybe it was more like forced proximity had stripped away all the non-essentials and at the core of it, he genuinely liked her. He'd always respected her—even when the fighting was dirty, she'd been a worthy opponent. But maybe the respect went further than that.

He knew for damn sure he was more than just attracted to her. He couldn't blame the pencil skirt for it any longer. He wanted her. Badly.

How bad would it really be if they just...gave in? They could get the inconvenient lust out of their systems. They were adults. It was obvious they would never be able to date once they got back to the city. Neither one of them would want to. He wasn't her type. Birk was her type.

But if they didn't give in now, they might always wonder. And that couldn't be good for their working relationship, right? The sexual tension would get in the way of work. So really, having sex at summer camp would be the best thing they could do for their company. He'd be doing Mr. Martin a favor.

Yeah. They'd be doing it for their company.

"We're lucky bastards, eh Miguel?"

Miguel turned to find Brad standing next to him now and watching the backsides of the women as they walked away.

Alliance, he reminded himself. Punching the guy would not be conducive to his goal. But he really wanted to. "Yeah. Being married is great."

"Layla convince Sera to join us later yet?"

Miguel tensed. "No. We have plans." *Plans that do not include you ogling my wife's naked body, asshole.* Though, if he had his way, he'd be ogling her naked body tonight in the cabin. His idea was sounding better all the time. Their approach had been all wrong. Instead of fighting the feelings, they should just have given in to them that first night. All the time they'd been wasting...

"She's shy then?" Brad interrupted Miguel's thoughts. "Maybe a few more drinks. Know what I mean?"

It took Miguel a minute to figure out where the conversation had gone while he'd been mentally undressing Sera. Was Brad suggesting he get his wife drunk so she'd agree to skinny dipping? His protective urges were brought to the surface. He wasn't brought up to take advantage of women that way. "No, man. We're just…"

"What do you think of Layla?" Brad interrupted. "She's hot right?"

What kind of question was that? Was there a proper way to answer it? Because Miguel didn't think so. *Yeah, your wife is hot* didn't sound right. Neither did, *No not really*. Mostly, he didn't have any interest in Brad's wife aside from maybe her vote for best couple. If there even was a vote. He really hated not knowing the parameters of the competition. "Layla is very nice."

After a long, measured look, Brad took another drink. "She's a little wild sometimes. When we go on vacation, she likes to let off some steam."

Play dumb, Castillo.

"She's a good wife. I don't mind her having a good time. You can't keep a wild bird in a cage, know what I mean?"

"I don't think I do, Brad. And I think I'm okay with that."

Brad smiled. "You ever wonder what it would be like to see your wife with another—"

"Here they come." Something was happening inside him. He wasn't sure he liked it. It was one thing to have a fun romp with Sera. It was another to have all these caveman feelings. But there they were, bubbling up inside his blood. Sera was his woman. His. And if Brad didn't shut the hell up, Miguel was going to charge him like a buck in spring. "Like I said, we have plans tonight, but you guys have a good time. Catch you later, bro." Miguel trotted up the trail to meet the women. "Babe, we need to get going. Have a good night, Layla."

He captured Sera's hand and jogged back up the trail toward their cabin. He was about two seconds away from grunting, "Me man. You woman."

"Miguel, slow down."

He turned to her, unsure what his problem was other than the idea of someone else touching her made him crazy. It should have been hot, right? A threesome? A foursome? But no. It didn't make him hot. It didn't make him bothered. It made him want to hide her away. And that made no sense because she wasn't his.

Shit. He wanted her to be his.

They began walking again. Slower this time. "What's gotten in to you?"

"Nothing."

He took the cabin steps two at a time and opened the door. He wanted to put her in a fireman hold and get her into the cabin, away from everyone but him. He wanted to do things to her that would ensure she screamed his name. He wanted things from Sera he hadn't wanted in a long time.

"I think Layla has a crush on you," she said, breezing past him like he wasn't just this side of losing control completely. "She talked about you the whole time we were in the bathroom. Why are you staring at me like that?"

Because standing there in the middle of the room, the soft glow of the lamp behind her, her hair in a messy bun that looked like it might have marshmallow stuck in it, and wearing his oldest flannel shirt, she was the most beautiful woman he'd ever seen.

"Miguel?"

He took a step toward her, closing the distance. "I think her crush is more on you, but I don't want to talk about Layla."

"Okay." She squinted. "Why do I feel like you're about to pounce on me?"

"Because I am."

IF SHE'D JUST MET MIGUEL this evening, Sera would never have believed him to be the same man she worked with in the city. It wasn't just the beginnings of a beard or the worn jeans. Miguel in the city was laid back and loose limbed even in suits and ties and polished shoes. Miguel in the woods was tense, like a jaguar ready to spring, despite his casual attire.

He was need honed to a fine edge. A predator eying his next meal. She felt vaguely uneasy—not because he would devour her but because part of her wanted him to. The gnawing ache inside her demanded it.

His intentions were clear. He didn't have to voice them. Standing in front of her was Grade A primal male ready to take his mate. "This is a very bad idea." She didn't name off all the reasons. They been down this path before and nothing had changed except that look in his eye.

"I don't think it matters anymore, princess. You're going to have to tell me to leave if you don't want this because I can't spend another night in this cabin without exploring every inch of you with my tongue."

Liquid heat pooled between her legs. "Oh," was all she could say. Because she was stuck on the picture of his words. She hadn't figured him for a dirty talker. She hadn't figured to like it so much.

One step closer, in her space, yet not. "I'm going to start with that patch behind your ear, Sera, because I know that turns your knees to jelly."

He was wrong. He didn't have to touch her to turn her knees to jelly. Just his voice was doing a damn good job of it.

Behind her now, he continued a slow circle. There was an intense static between their bodies, like an electrical current was going to arc, zapping them both. "I'm dying to taste you. I want to scrape my tongue over your nipples and finally know the weight of your breasts in my hand."

She should be talking. Saying something. Stopping him before this went any further. Before it went too far. But that damned gnawing ache grew larger, spreading over her limbs and weighing down her tongue so she couldn't speak. Afraid if she opened her mouth, the only thing that would sound would be a desperate keening, she waited as he circled back to her front.

"You're not sending me away. Why is that?" One fingertip traced a feather light line from her temple to her jaw. She shivered, showing her weakness. This was crazy. He'd barely touched her. "Do you think I'm bluffing? Because I'm not. I'm not sure what you've done to me, but I promise I intend to return the favor. You won't know yourself anymore. I'm going to turn you inside out, Sera. Just like you've done to me. Over and over. This marriage gets consummated tonight." His hand slid to her neck, feeling where her pulse hammered wildly. "Unless you send me away." He leaned down until they were eye to eye. "Are you going to send me away, princess?"

"I can't breathe."

"Yes you can. Tell me to go."

"I can't…"

He took a step back and she grasped the front of his t-shirt. "Don't go. Stay."

His already dark eyes turned even more so. "You're mine. I don't know what happens next week, but the rest of camp, you're mine."

She nodded, mute in the intensity of his gaze. She wasn't going to think about next week. She loosened her hold on the front of his shirt so she could grab the hem. He helped get it over his head, and then her hands roamed the expanse of delicious male chest. She didn't question his possessive demand since she felt it too. "You're mine also, Castillo." She wrapped her arms around him, stroking his strong back. Muscles bunched and tensed under her caresses. She wanted to touch him everywhere.

"Agreed." He reached for the hair band, letting loose the messy bun. "In my dreams, your hair is always down like this."

She angled her head. "You dream about me?"

"More than I care to admit. Get naked."

She placed a kiss to the soft patch of hair in the center of his chest, gratified by the involuntary shiver she received in return. So she kissed an inch lower while his large hands tunneled through her hair.

"I said get naked."

"Busy." Sera pressed lower, a groan her reward. She tongued a path back up, circling his flat nipple.

Miguel flipped her around, her back to his chest.

"Hey." She tried to squirm, but he held her strong.

"Nope." His hand slipped beneath the waistband of her jeans. "Sometimes you need to let me lead, remember?" His finger touched the top of her sex and he buried his nose in her hair to suck on the patch of skin below her ear. As promised. "I won't take you anywhere you don't want to go."

She arched, trying to bring his hand into further contact. "If you do this half as well as you mambo—oh." Direct contact with his fingers cut off whatever it was she was going to say.

Miguel chuckled, but brought his hand back out of her pants. "Get naked, Worth. I'm not going to tell you again."

"Or what?"

He spun her back around, grabbed the lapels of the flannel shirt and rent it down the middle, the buttons skittering off the wood floor. He pushed it down over her shoulders, trapping her arms, and walked her backward toward the bed. "That's what."

"It was your shirt anyway."

"I'll give you another one."

When the backs of her knees hit the mattress, he pushed her gently until she was on her backside, propped up on her elbows. Then he went to work on her socks and shoes. When she tried to sit up to work her arms free, he held her still. "I'm leading right now."

Was she willing to keep her arms trapped while he did whatever he wanted to her? Yeah, she so was. "Will I get a turn to lead later?"

"Darling, you can have as many turns as you want." He undid her jeans, directed her to move her hips, and slid the denim down her legs, panties and all. She should have felt self-conscious, but as he moved his strong hands firmly back up her calves and thighs, his eyes staring at her, she lost the desire to keep any inhibitions.

There was no point.

She let her head fall back when he nuzzled at her mound. After he placed an almost chaste kiss there, he said, "I'd rather you watched me."

She lifted her head and questioned him with a look.

"Oh yeah, I love it when you arch one brow at me. You do that at the office all the time." Miguel widened her legs, settling in at the juncture of her thighs. "I want you to watch me. I want you to watch me turn you inside out."

He licked her slowly and she struggled to keep her eyes from falling closed in bliss. He paused, making eye contact with her and once again he reminded her of a wild cat. A jaguar going in for the kill. Using his fingers to separate the lips of her sex, he used his whole mouth on her. Driving her to peak after peak, yet she hadn't yet crested. She couldn't hold up her head anymore. She couldn't hold onto a thought anymore. Her world reduced to Miguel and his mouth.

"Come for me, Sera."

She wanted to. Oh god, she wanted to. But she couldn't let go. There was still that part of her, that rigid unyielding part, that wanted to hold her back. "I can't…"

"Yes, you can." One hand slipped up her belly and under the tank top she had forgotten she still wore. He groaned when he got a handful of her braless-breast, and then he pulled his hand out enough to push the whole shirt up and over her breasts. She felt so wanton, half dressed and spread open for him. Once again, she thought she might go over the edge. She was straining for something out of reach.

"I really can't…"

"Yes, you can." Miguel pinched her nipple while rolling his tongue over her and she came without warning. Waves of pleasure crashed over her, and he stayed with her until they ebbed, leaving her wrung out and shaking. She felt the cold when he moved away, heard the rasp of his zipper and pants as they came down his legs. The next sound was a wrapper for condoms she didn't know were in the room, and then he was on top of her suckling her neck.

"You're amazing. Beautiful. I love the way you taste. The way you look when you come."

Sera wrapped her legs around him, wishing her arms were free, and drew him closer, trying to get him inside. He felt so good, his skin sliding against hers, the hard length of him heavy against her stomach. He raised up, holding himself above her while he slid into her with one powerful stroke, his eyes never leaving her.

He filled her completely. She felt him everywhere.

In and out so slowly she thought she might die, he kept his rhythm and his eye contact until the tendons in his neck stretched tautly, giving him away. He was losing control and she couldn't wait until he tumbled off the cliff.

He paused, resting his forehead on hers, his eyes watching her. She'd never felt so open. Never felt the need to be so open. So exposed. She wanted him to take her wherever he wanted to go.

She planted her feet and arched into him, pushing him deeper.

"Oh god. Sera, you're killing me."

"So you don't want me to do it again?" she asked, even as she did it.

"Fuck." He reached between them and put direct pressure on her again. "I'm not going until you do."

She bucked against him because she had no choice. Everything felt so damn good. "I already went, remember?"

"Again, Sera." Miguel stroked her as a raw, low sound escaped him. It was that sound that put her over the edge. That tugged on the invisible cords in her center. She came again, contracting around him as he gave one last thrust and followed her.

CHAPTER SIX

> **Good morning, Campers!**
>
> Pastry chef Allison and our dance instructor Sue are teaming up for a two-part class today and tomorrow—Meringue and Merengue—learn a dessert and a dance this week! They'll be in the boathouse at 4 p.m. each day.
>
> We also have a special on hot stone massages and a midnight nature walk. Meet at the archery field at 11:50 for that.
>
> **Day Five**
> Sunrise Yoga: 7:30 a.m.
> Softball game: 10 a.m.-11 a.m.
> Counseling: 1 p.m. ~~2 p.m.~~ 1:50
> Arts & Crafts: 2:30 p.m. to 3:30 p.m.
> Massage: 4 p.m.

SERA WOKE UP ALONE.

Maybe it wasn't really a surprise. It's not like they talked about what would happen to their "relationship" after they had sex. Because until last night, sex hadn't been a foregone conclusion.

Or had it?

Maybe it had been assured the moment they'd stepped into the cabin and realized they'd be sharing a bed for a week. Maybe she'd been foolish to think she could control the situation. Because sex with Miguel was out of control. Scary out of control. Or at least it should have been.

Sera wasn't a prude. She liked sex. Had liked sex a little too much and probably too often in college—but she'd always been careful. Not just with condoms, but with her heart. She'd chosen her sexual partners very carefully, even then. And the last few years, she'd only slept with men who were likely to make good partners for the next phase of her life too. It was time to start thinking about long-term. If she wanted to have a child, and she thought she probably did, she needed to start planning.

Miguel was so not in her plans.

She rolled over until she was on his pillow. It smelled like him, so she inhaled deeply. Which was ridiculous. He'd slipped out of their cabin before sunrise to avoid her. It made no sense to moon over him like a lovesick teenager.

But really, it was hardly her fault he smelled so good.

Sera stretched. Deliciously sore and a little tender. Miguel had done a good job last night, and she refused to regret what happened. She couldn't take it back, and she didn't want to anyway. If he was feeling weird this morning, that was on him.

She'd suspected they would be good together in bed just because he was so wrong for her. But he was also sure of his body. And who knew she liked a caveman in the bedroom. She tried to imagine someone like Phillip telling her to come and it made her giggle.

When the door opened, she sat up, surprised to see Miguel juggling the door and a cardboard flat. Before she could get out of bed to help him, he said, "Do not get up." He kicked the door closed and laughed. "Do you practice that eyebrow thing in the mirror?"

"Yes."

"Well, your practice has paid off."

"Why can't I get up?"

"Because you look amazing and I'm coming back to that bed right now with gifts." He set the flat down, kicked off his shoes, and stripped.

"Are you supposed to be my gift? Shouldn't I be the one to unwrap you?"

"Sera Worth, you are a naughty girl."

Naked now, he turned to grab the tray and she stared at his ass. Yes, he was a gift all right. He turned again and made a clucking sound when he caught her staring. He was blocking her view of his other parts with the box he brought with him to bed.

"I kept you up so late last night, I thought the least I could do was bring you coffee before yoga." He handed her a cup, two creams, and a sugar. He'd been paying attention. Then he pulled out a Styrofoam box, making a big production of opening it like it was a ring box. "Sera Worth, my counterfeit bride, will you have breakfast with me?"

"Is that chocolate? Where did you get it?" The confection was the signature dessert from dinner last night. Camp Firefly Falls did not skimp on the chefs they brought in and the pastry chef was a goddess. This dessert was called The Firefly and they'd had it the first night too. It was worth coming to camp for.

He handed her a fork. "I snuck into the kitchen."

"You stole it?"

"I might have used my considerable charm to be given a piece."

"You flirted with the chef to bring me chocolate? You must really care."

He took the fork from her hand and fed her a piece. Pure bliss. "Actually, when I snuck in to get the coffee, I found one of the owners in there. I promised not to tell his wife he was sneaking dessert if he let me bring you back some."

"So you committed blackmail for me. I'm touched."

"Not yet, but as soon as you finish that chocolate you will be. Though I'm starting to wonder if I can compete. You really like that dessert, don't you?"

She thought about breaking out her Meg Ryan impression to show him just how much she liked the dessert, but decided to just keep eating.

They ate and drank their coffee in silence. At least until the silence began to feel heavy.

He cleared his throat. Twice. "Do we need to talk about last night?"

"Are you fishing for compliments, Castillo?"

He set the empties on the nightstand. "I appreciate you trying to keep things light—but I also know you. Last night wasn't the plan, and you don't like going off plan."

"Not generally, no. I know that come Monday, our lives go back to normal. We don't make sense in the real world, but this isn't the real world. And we do make sense here. It's business. We want to win this account, so we need to sell this campaign, right? Nothing says we can't also enjoy it."

He pulled her to his chest. "I am enjoying it. I don't ever want to get married in real life—but I like Camp Miguel and Camp Sera. They are a nice couple. I say we let them have the next few days. Monday will sort itself out."

She snuggled in a little more. "Camp Sera thinks that's a great idea."

Sera ignored the warning siren blaring in her head. She could handle this for three more days. It would be like...playing a part in a movie.

No problem.

SITTING ACROSS FROM BIRK FELT a bit like being called to the principal's office for some reason.

"We missed you two at yoga this morning."

Sera stole a glance at Miguel and felt a blush grow hot on her cheeks. They'd been busy. Working on their "campaign."

"We slept in," Miguel answered.

Birk leaned back in his chair. "Well, it is vacation, right?" He winked like they weren't fooling anyone. Except that they were fooling everyone. Themselves most of all, but she'd think about that later. "Today, we're going to learn techniques for diffusing arguments when discussing hard topics. As you've said, you don't have any rough spots right now—but these will come in handy in the future and work just as well with anyone, not just marital communications. You can use these techniques at work too. If you have any issues with co-workers."

Oh, he had no idea.

He went on to explain using "I statements" instead of "you statements."

"Let's practice. Sera, we are going to role-play. You are ready to start a family, but Miguel won't talk to you about it."

She took a deep breath and remembered the tips he'd just told them, refreshing herself with the pamphlet. Miguel snorted at her attempts to be prepared. He would. She set down the paper. "Honey, since we are finally having a quiet night at home without a lot of things pulling us in different directions, I'd like to talk about starting a family."

Playing along with the role-play, Miguel answered, "Sera, I think we should enjoy this quiet night and make the most of this time. We don't get quiet nights at home very often."

"I know, sweetheart. I specifically set this evening up so we would have no distractions. It's important to me that I have your full attention." That line was straight out of the pamphlet.

"I'd love to give you my full attention. Let's start with a glass of wine in the hot tub."

He was deflecting. With sex. She had a feeling that might be how he'd deflect discussions if they were really in a relationship.

Which of course would never happen.

"If we start in the hot tub, we'll get off track." She imagined that Camp Miguel and Camp Sera liked to sit in the hot tub naked. They seemed like that kind of couple. "Why don't we talk first and then have that wine."

"I'm really not in the mood for a heavy discussion."

"It doesn't have to be heavy."

He tensed, play acting came very naturally to him. Not so much for her. "I already know what you are going to say. You want a baby. I'm not ready."

"Don't put words in my mouth."

Or maybe it did. Maybe just arguing with him came very naturally to her.

"Am I wrong?"

"Well, no."

"Then let's table it for now."

"I don't want to table it. You always do that!"

Birk interrupted, "Remember to use 'I statements' Sera. They are less likely to put Miguel on the defense."

She was about to tell Birk where he could put his 'I statement' when she remembered they weren't really fighting. That this was a game. Right?

"What do I always do?" Miguel wanted to know.

"You table it. Is it so hard to just tell me how you are feeling?"

"You aren't listening to how I'm feeling."

Birk held up a hand. "I statement."

Miguel looked about as happy with Birk as she was. "My feelings about having a baby haven't changed. I'm not ready. I told you I didn't think I'd ever be ready. But that isn't good enough, is it?"

"I just want to know why." He'd be a great dad. She could see him coaching his kids about baseball like he did with her.

"No you don't. You just want me to change my mind." He shot Birk a glare, daring him to interject. "We talked about this before we got married. I told you then I didn't think I'd ever want kids. You said you were okay with that."

"Is that why you didn't marry *her*?"

Miguel's face lost color for a moment and then got red. "Excuse me?"

She wished she could take it back, but it was already out there. "You told me you had asked someone to marry you before me. Is this what broke you up?"

"We are *not* talking about her." His voice was so cold. So not Mr. Fun. Mr. Everybody Loves Me.

"Why? Why can't we ever talk about her?"

Poor Birk. "You guys are getting a little off topic. While I think this is opening up a dialogue about things you need to discuss, it's not the exercise we're working on."

She didn't think Miguel even heard Birk. "She has no place in this or any conversation. Let it go, Sera."

"You don't get to just put up that kind of wall. I deserve to know why you didn't get married. I'm your wife."

"Are you listening to yourself here? You *are* my wife. She is not. She doesn't have a place in this conversation."

"Did she want kids?"

"Yes."

"Is that why you broke up?"

"No."

"Why didn't you marry her then?"

Miguel stood up. "I did."

"What?"

"I married her. We were married for three days and then she died. Can we let this go now?"

THAT WAS NOT SUPPOSED TO happen.

As soon as the words were out of Miguel's mouth, he wanted to take them back, swallow them back down to where he'd been keeping them all these years. Never ever utter them again. The white hot rage left him as soon as the words did, and now all he was left with was a hollow ache and regret.

He sat back down.

"I'm sorry...I didn't know." Sera reached for his hand and then snatched hers back when he glared at her. He reached over and squeezed her knee in apology. "I shouldn't have pushed."

Birk leaned forward in his chair, coldly assessing them both. "So you've never talked about your first marriage to Sera, Miguel?"

"I don't talk about it with anyone." He settled back into his chair, defeated. "Nobody else knows. Well, the hospital chaplain and the two nurses know, I guess."

"You married her in a hospital," Sera deduced. "And then she died?"

He scrubbed his hands over his face. His parents didn't even know. Not even after all this time. They'd learned to not bring her up—and since he certainly never did, the three-day marriage was moot.

"Bria was literally the girl next door. We'd been dating throughout high school." Why was he telling her this? "We had a lot of plans. We'd been accepted to the same college, were going to get married and settle down in our hometown after we got teaching degrees." Sera raised her eyebrow. Teaching was a long way from business and marketing. "I wanted to teach middle school. Bria talked about teaching for a few years and going back for a higher degree. She wanted to be a principal. We knew what street we wanted to live on, how many kids we wanted to have." He closed his eyes. "Three." When he opened them, Sera had tears in hers. "And then she got sick. We had our entire lives planned out." He thought Sera would get a kick out of that. That he used to be a planner.

"Miguel, you don't have to—"

"When she got so sick that we knew she wasn't leaving the hospital again, we wanted one thing from that future that was never going to be. Just one thing. So we got married in the hospital. And I didn't tell anyone. And when she was gone, I stopped planning out my life and just concentrated on living it."

He was sure Birk was enjoying this show—a rare chink in their marital armor. But he was quiet. Watching them both. Watching as Sera eased her way into Miguel's lap to offer comfort. Watching as Miguel tensed at first, then held her close. Listening as she murmured nonsensical words that shouldn't have been necessary after all this time.

It should have been worse that Birk witnessed this, but Miguel was glad he was there. If it had been just Sera, he might have cracked completely, but falling apart in front of Birk was not an option.

Why was falling apart in front of Sera not out of the question?

He was sure he was some kind of textbook case for the counselor. Young boy loses his young love. Instead of being overwhelmed with grief, he goes the opposite way. Party all the time. That's what he'd done.

He'd calmed down since college, of course, but Miguel barely remembered his first two years. If there was a prank, he was in on it. If there was a party, he was the center of it. If there was a pretty girl—well, he went through a lot of them in his younger days. Anything to numb the pain.

His parents had tried to rein him in—offering trite advice about what Bria would have wanted for him. But Miguel didn't care. Bria was gone. His whole world was gone. And he'd vowed to never hurt like that again.

No marriage. No kids. Just work and play. Yeah, it was a shallow existence. But it was a painless one.

He tried to imagine what it would be like to really be married to Sera and lose her like he had lost Bria all those years ago. He didn't think he could go through that again. But as she curled into his arms, overwhelming all his senses, he wondered if a better man would try.

CHAPTER SEVEN

> **Good morning, Campers**
>
> Don't forget the field trip to Briarsted today. Bus leaves at nine a.m. If you have a softball game today, you can catch the tour tomorrow.
>
> **Day Six**
> Softball: 10 a.m.
> Canoe trip to Elephant Rock: 1 p.m.
> Arts & Crafts: 4 p.m.

HE WAS QUIET. IN HIS own world. Thrown back into a dark corner—the darkest corner—of his life, and she'd been the one to toss him there.

Sera wasn't even sure how the counseling session had gotten so far away from them. It had felt like a game at first—role-play these two people in this marriage that doesn't exist. But something had flipped inside her. A bad switch. She felt his reticence to commit to a child like it was a personal attack on her. Which was ridiculous. What was it about him that brought out the worst in her? She shuddered when she remembered the last six months. How awful she'd been to him. How awful he'd been to her. Things were different now, after they'd decided to work together. After they'd had sex.

So what made her want to dig in so hard during their mock communication exercise?

They'd been on eggshells ever since the counseling session yesterday. Oh, they'd gone to their couples' massage, their softball game, the campfire—but they'd been shadows of Camp Miguel and Camp Sera. Going through the motions, but not committing. Not fully.

And while they'd slept together last night—they didn't have sex.

Holding hands for show, they walked down to the dock for yoga, taking their usual spot on the mats. Miguel said it was important that Birk see them together, and maybe he was right.

It was cooler today. The sunrise taking its time to push through the clouds. Maybe it wouldn't manage today. It smelled like it had rained last night. Maybe they'd get some more. It certainly went with her mood.

"We're going to do a new pose today," Essa said in her steady, calming voice. "Yab Yum is about divine unity. It will allow you to align your chakras—but for those of you not interested in the meditation or woo-woo benefits—it also just feels really good. We'll have the bigger partner cross legged like Birk is doing. Then the smaller partner will sit on the lap like this." She climbed on to him and crossed her legs behind Birk's back. "Once you sit Yab Yum, it is really up to you how to continue. You want your eyes aligned, but you may simply close them and breathe together."

Oh shit.

Miguel sat, crossing his legs as best he could—and it was certainly better than their first yoga session. She eased down over him, settling with their groins aligned. Their eyes locked. It should have been too intimate, but it still didn't feel close enough.

"Lean your foreheads together and close your eyes. Take a few deep breaths and then just be, allowing yourself to synchronize to your partner."

Just be. Did she even know how to do that?

He was sturdy. So sturdy. She rested against him, trying to keep the wall around herself in this very intimate pose. Trying not to sink too far. But it wasn't long before they were breathing as one.

In. Out. In. Out.

Part of her was reaching for him even as she tried to stop it. But he felt like the sun and she was craving warmth.

She opened her eyes to find him focused on her. His arms tightened, pulling her closer. The hard length of him pressed into her. And he smiled.

"I'm so sorry," she whispered. Willing him to understand she hadn't wanted to rip him apart, no matter how it seemed.

He shook his head. "Shh. It's okay."

Meditation had always seemed out of her reach. She understood it on a basic level, and it was gaining popularity in the corporate world along with buzz words that wouldn't last long. Like "forty-hour work week." But people were trying to find a balance. She'd just never been able to think of nothing. It was jarring—almost scary—the few times she'd tried. But for ten minutes, she was able to sit chakra to chakra with Miguel, focusing only on their breath, the sound of the water lapping against the supports of the deck, the breeze. Like they had a bubble. Around them, the worries of things said and unsaid might be swirling around, trying to permeate their cocoon of silence—but for the first time, she was able to let it go.

"Let's just concentrate on Camp Miguel and Camp Sera for the next two days. Can we do that?" he asked. "I'll even make you a sandwich."

Sera giggled and vowed to just *be*. No past. No future. Just live in the moment.

She didn't know what happened come Monday. What they would take with them from this experience. But she knew what she'd leave here at Camp Firefly Falls.

A piece of her heart. One she couldn't afford to lose.

Later that afternoon

MIGUEL WOULDN'T CALL IT NAPPING. His eyes were open, he was aware, but it's like his body was unconscious. The sex they'd just had…crazy good. Too good. Maybe even unreal good.

"We live here now," Sera said from her position of being sprawled over his chest. "I'm too tired to ever leave."

The Yab Yumming on the dock that morning had started a sensation in him that he couldn't just push down. All day, he'd wanted to get it back. That perfect feeling. That unity.

But they'd had softball, lunch, and then a canoe trip to Elephant Rock. Sitting behind her in the canoe, watching the play of her back and shoulder muscles, had been difficult enough that he'd carried her back to their cabin from the boathouse and they'd been naked ever since.

Sera rolled away onto her side, but it was too far. He kissed her shoulder, her neck. The hollow of her throat intoxicated him. "Too tired." She flopped onto her stomach.

"I don't think you are."

"You're insatiable, Castillo. Do we have any food in here?"

"No."

"Go get me a sandwich."

He laughed and kissed her strong back, trailing down until he got to a pink scar, which he also kissed, following it around her side under her breast. "What is this. Shark attack?"

She stiffened. "Something like that."

He remembered registering the mark briefly the other night and again this afternoon. But it was light in color and looked more like a scratch. He traced it with his finger. "Tell me."

He wanted to hear a story about her childhood. About little Princess Seraphina getting into some kind of trouble. She couldn't always have been as careful and controlled as she was today.

"It's from my surgeries. My heart surgeries. I had coarctation of the artery when I was a kid. I was born with it. It's a heart defect."

He pulled back. Momentarily stunned. "Surgeries? You've had *multiple* heart surgeries?" The medicine bottle in their shared bathroom made an appearance in his memory. "Are you still sick?"

He remembered all the medicine Bria had taken daily. Most of it to counteract the side effects from other medicines she had to take. His vision constricted and noise started fading to the background. He tried to blink away the sensation from the blood leaving his head.

"No, not really. Not anymore."

He remembered the pink curtain around Bria's hospital bed. The exact sound the rings made when the nurse would slide it closed when she took care of the catheter. The plastic pitcher on the nightstand, always full of ice chips. The basin, always ready for the next attack of Bria's nausea. He closed his eyes. "What do you mean not really?"

The memories came flying back to him. Bria hadn't wanted to die in a hospital gown, so he'd helped her into ducky pajamas. They were two sizes too big by that stage of her illness.

"Well, as long as I take care of myself and get frequent checkups, then I'm fine."

His hand tightened on her arm. "What would a bad checkup be?"

"I guess if they found heart enlargement on the ECHO or other cardiac testing. I wouldn't *want* to have another heart surgery—it's a little more major now than when I was a kid—but it's not like I'd have much choice. But I can't dwell on it. I just take good care of myself and make sure to see my doctor. It's why I'm so organized."

Heart surgery? Lunch was threatening to come back up.

He couldn't. Not again.

God, he'd just found her. If he lost her now...

But worse...what if he lost her a year from now? Ten years? What if they had a kid?

A life he didn't know he wanted flashed before his eyes and all of it could be gone in a blink if she had a bad checkup. Just like the plans he'd made once before.

He knew better. He'd perfected knowing better for years.

The cloying smell of carnations. The way the light from the stained glass hit Bria's waxy skin in her coffin.

He got up, started gathering his clothes. "We might be missing something that will help us win the grand prize. We should get back out there."

She sat up, her brow wrinkled in confusion. She looked beautiful wrapped up in a sheet, her skin still red where his beard had scraped her. "Miguel?"

But he couldn't face her. Not right now. Not like this.

"Sera...I'm sorry."

"Sorry for what exactly?"

"I think I pushed us too fast. I'm not ready. I thought maybe…next week…but no. This won't work. It can't work. We should stop this right now before one of us gets the wrong idea about what is happening here."

"Don't flatter yourself, Castillo." Sera lost all the color in her face as her too smart mind started catching up with the conversation. "My scars freaked you out."

"No, of course not." He needed to bring back the fun, easy going vibe. "We should hit the Arts and Crafts session. See what kinky things we can make today."

"It's my heart defect then. Miguel, it's not a big deal."

"I just think we're getting too cozy. All this forced togetherness. We're really good at what we do, and we are selling the hell out of this marriage. But we need to make sure we don't become our target consumer, you know?"

She balked. "You think I can't tell the difference between what is real and what is fantasy."

No. He was pretty sure that he was the one who couldn't tell. "You're getting uppity again."

"Uppity?" Most women would have screeched the question. Not his wife. No, her voice was cool, polished. Icy. "I see."

She wrapped the sheet around herself and walked coolly to the bathroom. She didn't slam the door. No. Just a quiet snick of the lock. And then the shower started. She was washing him off of her.

Miguel sat on the bed, not sure how things had gotten so out of control. This wasn't like him. And putting it all back on her was a total dick move.

A real man would apologize. Would not make her feel at fault or self-conscious about her health. A real man would do a lot of things that Miguel hadn't been able to do. Sera wasn't the only one with a heart defect.

"I'm so sorry, Sera," he said, even though she couldn't hear him. "I don't have the heart to love you."

THERE WAS PEACE IN A certain kind of numbness.

Sera found it as she surveyed their shared cabin and realized Miguel had packed and was gone.

The numbing started as an icy cold pain, but working like Novocain, the pain soon blurred into a fuzzy sensation in her chest.

She'd nearly lost her heart to him, hadn't she?

Sera sank into the chair where she'd sat when they first masterminded their marriage campaign. It was only a few days ago. Less than a week. How had everything changed so much that nothing was different now?

She was alone. As alone as she'd been when they'd gotten here.

Miguel hadn't changed either. He was just as unpredictable and unreliable as the man she knew from the city. It was her own fault she'd bought into their marketing. Damn, he was good, wasn't he? He should have won the director position. She didn't have half his talent for effective promotional message delivery.

He'd sold her a concept. Instead of pitching to the camp staff—he'd made *her* the lead influencer. When she bought in, everyone else would follow, right?

And boy, she'd bought in. She wanted to be Mrs. Miguel because Mrs. Miguel wasn't lonely. She didn't have to worry about everything all by herself. She had a partner. For the first time since she was a child, she didn't have to carry all the responsibility. Her life, the fictional woman they'd made up, was simple and happy. Her husband adored her. What had he said? He couldn't wait to come home to her.

They were going to raise agnostic heathens together.

The first tear came when she realized that the kitchen renovations they'd planned while sitting in a canoe today were never going to happen. She was never going to have a dog like Fido. What would she do with a dog right now? She worked ten and twelve-hour days and lived alone.

Pull yourself together.

The ice princess he'd accused her of being so many times would not cry over a fictional life. She was smart and practical. Somehow, she had to pull this one out of the campfire—just because he'd left didn't mean she couldn't win the grand prize.

It was almost time for the pre-dinner cocktail hour. She'd walk in with her head held high. No one would see her upset. Miguel…she'd say he had a business emergency in the city. She was staying behind to relax and read and enjoy the last day of their vacation. No sense in both of them paying for airline ticket changes.

She splashed cold water on her face. Skipped the flannel shirt he'd left in the closet for her, putting on her own instead.

She looked at her ring finger. Tomorrow night, she could move the ring back to her right hand. Where it belonged.

She got to the door and stopped, sliding to the floor.

She willed the numbness back. She didn't want these feelings.

He'd made her believe. Maybe he was right. Maybe she couldn't tell the difference between reality and fantasy.

Or maybe he'd set her up. Done this on purpose.

She'd never thought him to be mean spirited. Sure there were times when they'd both been devious during the run at the promotion—but they were supposed to be on the same side now at camp.

Nothing made sense. Her heart, the stupid naive thing it was, sank lower as the numbness continued to wear off.

Revenge. That had to be it. He was so upset about not winning the promotion that he'd orchestrated a way to bring her down. It wasn't about winning the grand prize or convincing everyone they were a happy couple. For Miguel, it had always been about revenge. Getting her in his bed wasn't enough. He'd wanted her to hurt. To feel things. He calculated every move so carefully. Earned her trust. Made her fall. Held out to her everything she secretly desired. Then yanked it back like a bully and laughed at her.

Her heart was already defective. She'd be damned if she allowed him to break it too.

City Miguel may have bested her this time, but she could grind Camp Miguel into the dust.

She dug through her makeup bag for the first time since they'd gotten to camp. Undid one more button on the shirt. Pocketed a condom from the box he'd left behind.

Tonight, she cheated on her husband.

CHAPTER EIGHT

THE COUPLE NEXT TO MIGUEL on the plane that evening was probably in their seventies. They shared a common shorthand language, honed by what was probably years of togetherness. They seemed to have a little ritual for getting settled in their seats. She held his book while he adjusted the pocket in front of him with what he'd need for the flight. Once he was buckled, she had an elaborate tray ritual in which she laid everything out the way she thought it might go after take-off, then rearranged it back into her bag, which her husband held in his lap without being asked. There was passing back and forth of ear plugs, gum, antacids. All without words. He wondered if they ever went on Rediscover Marital Intimacy getaways. Was that a thing a lot of couples did, or was that a product of the times?

If Bria had lived, would she and Miguel go to them? They'd still be together, right?

He didn't know. He couldn't know. He was a different Miguel than the one Bria married. He'd splintered, left that kid to stay forever at a funeral for a wife no one knew he had. It had killed him that her maiden name was on the headstone, but he didn't tell anyone to change it. It probably would have killed her parents more to not have it. There had been enough death already.

Certainly he hadn't told his family, who had hovered around him nonstop from the funeral through graduation through summer to his first day in the dorm. He'd let them sardine can his life, but never told them how he really was. What he really felt. He shoved it down, stayed quiet, and when they left him on campus, he shed the old kid and became someone new.

Nobody at college had known he'd lost Bria. Nobody knew he had ever thought he'd be a teacher. They didn't know he had been a quiet kid. That he'd played sports in high school, but didn't go to parties. That he spent more time with his family than kids his own age. What they did know was that he was always ready for a pickup game. That he was always ready for a beer. A girl. A laugh. He was a popular drunk for the first two years, and after coming close to academic probation, a popular dude who sometimes drank the next two. He turned to business college for the money. Because he wanted to make enough to plant his ass in the sand on a beach when he retired. He'd believed in the Great Cheeseburger in Paradise deity and little else for most of his adult life.

Advertising had been a natural fit for him. It was high energy. Thinking on your feet. It wasn't structured—until he met Sera anyway.

Sera. Man did he screw that up.

He scrubbed his hands over his face. Monday was going to suck. Every day here on out was going to suck. Whoever said it was better to have loved and lost than never to have loved at all was an even bigger idiot than Miguel was.

The old woman patted his arm on the rest between them. "You remind me of my grandson."

"Yeah?" He'd be surprised if he did. The older couple were too Nordic to produce a swarthy Mexican, but she was sweet. Maybe someone in her family married someone tanner. "Why is that?"

"He's having woman troubles too."

He raised his eyes at that. "What makes you think I'm—"

"You have the look," the old guy next to her said. "We've seen it a time or two. Six strapping boys and too many grandsons to count."

"Fourteen and two great-grandchildren," she answered for him.

"I stand corrected. Not too many to count. But all boys. Lots of women trouble."

That's a lot of boys. "How long have you two been married?"

"Fifty-two years."

"That's quite an accomplishment." If half of all marriages end in divorce, what did they do that another couple wouldn't have? Would he still be married? "I don't know how you do it."

They both shrugged. And then the attendant did the safety announcement. And then the plane took off. And then the woman patted his sleeve. "So, the woman trouble?" She led him gently into an answer despite that he didn't know her.

He spent the flight telling two kindly strangers about Sera, about his teen marriage, about how he ran away from something great because he was too afraid to go through the idea of losing someone again. Therefore—losing her anyway.

The seatbelt lights came on and they announced the plane was getting ready for descent.

The old man leaned over his wife's lap. "You're a dumbass, Miguel."

"Howard!" his wife chastised.

"Well he is. It's not a secret. He knows it. Look at him." Howard shook his head. "Nothing is promised. Nothing. Not tomorrow, not ten years from now, not fifty-two years from now. You were a brave kid once—you married that girl knowing exactly what wasn't promised."

"I wasn't brave." *I was naive.*

"Of course you were," Howard said. "The man you are today would have left when that poor girl got diagnosed."

The words arrowed into his heart. A clean shot. "That's not true."

"Sure it is."

Howard's wife pat his arm again. "I don't know what they taught you at your intimacy camping trip, but real intimacy is every day. It's waking up because your spouse is snoring. It's pretending to care about baseball scores. It's grieving together. It's joy together. It's not exercises you can practice. You just have to commit to every day. That's all."

Was one week enough time to get used to counting on every day? He thought of what it was like to eat every meal with Sera. To wait for her to finish brushing her teeth so he could pee. The mundane parts of living in a small cabin with her.

He'd liked it. "I'm a dumbass."

"Yep," Howard added.

Damn it. He was trapped in a tin can in the sky and he had to get back. Now.

Howard and Lynn, he'd finally asked her name, entertained him with stories for the rest of the flight while they circled the runway. Probably to keep him from opening an exit and jumping back to Sera. Their stories were…sometimes boring. He couldn't wait to bore someone with stories about his life with Sera.

Miguel got off the plane and immediately bought a return ticket. A red-eye back to camp.

That flight he spoke to no one. He just went over the stupid way he'd left camp. What was wrong with him? Howard was right. The Miguel he was at eighteen had a been more of a man than he'd been recently. That kid stood by the person he loved.

Loved.

Yeah. That.

Miguel wasn't stupid. He may be hard-headed—he was definitely a dumbass—but he wasn't stupid. He was in love. He loved Seraphina Worth.

And he'd broken her heart.

She might not give him a second chance. He didn't deserve one. So, she would probably tell him no. That was okay. It had to be. He just wouldn't give up. She wouldn't expect that. He'd wear her down. He was fairly confident he could. She obviously had feelings for him, despite her better judgment. So, he would just not give up.

He'd finally found something worth fighting for. He was just going to have to show her that he meant to commit to every day.

Love was not going to be easy for him. It would be hard not comparing her heart problems to Bria's cancer. It would be hard to not slip into fatalist thinking. Or worse, go back to only caring about the moment and never the consequences.

Dude. He had a lot of growing up to do.

It was almost dawn when he pulled into the gravel lot of Camp Firefly Falls. He didn't think it would be wise to slip back into their cabin while she was sleeping, so he made peace with the idea of resting his weary bones in one of the chairs on the porch outside their door.

He was about five feet away from the porch when the door opened. A man slipped out and gently closed the door behind him. He turned slowly.

Birk.

Fucking Birk was sneaking out of his wife's cabin at dawn.

CHAPTER NINE

> **Good morning, Campers**
>
> It's our last full day of camp. Time to cram as many of the activities as you can into one day since you've probably been slacking the entire week. That's what vacations are for though. And unlike summer sleepaway camp from your youth—you don't have to say goodbye to your crush tonight. We hope you'll join us for a special end of the session party in the boathouse tonight.
>
> **Day Seven:**
> Not signed up for anything

A GHOST PASSED THROUGH MIGUEL. The ghost of the love he managed to kill before he even had it.

The cold, deep chill iced over everything inside him. And then was replaced with white hot rage.

"What. The. Fuck."

Birk looked around and came bouncing down the steps. "Miguel," he said quietly. "You came back."

"Yeah. I came back to find the fucking marriage counselor doing the walk of shame out of my wife's cabin. Is that what they teach you in Psych 101? Isn't that against some kind of code of ethics? Banging your married client?"

"Keep it down man. People are sleeping."

"Are you fucking kidding me with this right now?"

Birk clapped a hand on his shoulder. "Come on, let's at least get off the lawn."

Miguel ducked out of his grasp. "Don't touch me. Don't fucking touch me."

He knew he didn't like that guy. From the very first time he saw him. "What do you think your bosses are going to say about you banging your clients? You're supposed to be saving marriages, man."

"We both know you're not married."

At that moment, the door opened again. Sera, sleepy eyed and wrapped in the plaid quilt from the bed, stepped onto the porch. "Miguel?"

Birk put his beefy hand in the middle of Miguel's chest, stopping him from going toward her. "I think we all need a cool down."

Did he think Miguel was going to hurt her? Jesus.

If he was going to hurt anyone, it was Birk the marriage counselor.

She looked so small up there, wrapped up in that quilt. Small and sad. Did she feel guilty? She shouldn't. He'd practically pushed her into another man's arms.

But if he looked as devastated as she did, they were both in way over their heads.

He turned to storm away because he really needed to smash something and he wanted it to be Birk's nose. But somehow, Birk used enough "I statements" and other diffusing language to get him to meet in his office in ten minutes. When Miguel got there, he was greeted by the barely awake Michael and Heather Tully. Sera was the last to arrive.

"Miguel, I've briefed the owners on the situation," Birk said calmly after they all took seats.

"Is that what this is? A situation?" He looked to his friend, Michael. "He had sex with his client."

"Seriously?" This from Sera. Cool Sera who was yelling. "You have a lot of nerve even being upset." She sat all the way back in her chair. "Sorry, am I being uppity again?"

Oh man. He was such a jerk.

"Let me just say a few things so I can keep my job and nobody gets hurt any more than they already are," Birk said. "Nothing inappropriate happened last night. Sera was upset when Miguel left. We talked most of the night and then I left when she fell asleep." He directed a stern gaze to Miguel. "She was in no shape to be alone, so I stayed with her."

My fault.

Heather yawned. "I don't really understand why you guys are pretending you're married. I mean it's fine, I guess. It's not against the law or anything."

Miguel just stared at Sera from across the room. Watched her push her hair behind her ear. Realized neither of them wanted to explain.

So Birk filled them in.

"Wait. Grand prize? You thought it was a competition?" Heather asked. "Like a marriage game of some kind?"

"It's not a competition?" Sera asked.

This time, Tully answered. A little too glibly for Miguel's taste. "Ah no. The grand prize is awarded in a drawing on the last night. It's for a free session next year. Which I'm sure the two of you would love to come back for."

Well, somehow that was surprising and not, all at the same time. There wasn't a prize. There had never been a prize.

"Sera, I'm so sorry," Miguel said, more tired than he'd ever been. He'd forgotten how much emotions weigh.

"Why did you come back?" she asked.

Because I realized I'm in love with you. "Because I realized I was being a jerk."

She frowned. Was she disappointed? He doubted she would want to hear the real reason. "Well, we agree on something."

"CAN I TALK TO MY husband…I mean…Miguel… alone, please?" Sera asked the room full of people she felt bad about dragging into her personal business. Especially as messy as it was.

When the Tullys filed out gratefully, Birk stood in the doorway. He'd been a good friend last night. A good counselor. "I'm sorry that I put you in such an awkward position with your bosses, Birk. If they have any other questions, please tell them I'm willing to vouch for your professional behavior."

"You sure you're okay?"

She nodded, though she could feel the heat of Miguel seething behind her. When Birk was gone, she closed the door and turned to Miguel. "I don't owe you any explanations, but nothing happened with Birk."

"I believe you. And you don't owe me anything. I understand. I owe you an apology, though. I shouldn't have run."

"I thought you were playing me. That you slept with me for revenge."

"No, Sera, I swear. I was just…I don't know how to do this. I freaked out."

She shrugged. "I could have been a little more understanding. A lot of painful memories came bubbling to the surface for you this week. It's a lot to confront." She paused, steeling herself. "But it hurt."

"I could have taken a walk or gone for a swim. It was immature of me to run away."

She wasn't going to argue.

She sat next to him on the couch. He'd told her some hard truths. Reasons why he couldn't love again. It was maybe her turn to do the same. Clear the air. Their marriage was doomed from the start because they would never have mature enough hearts to make it work with anyone, much less each other. "My mom is a really nice, loving person. But she's not a very sensible one. She's got some mental issues that weren't conducive to raising a special needs child. She tried very hard and she's high functioning most of the time—but a lot of it is dependent on meds and she hates taking them."

"That must have been hard on you growing up."

Sera nodded. "I had to grow up quickly. And I learned to be very careful from a very young age." Too young. Too careful.

"We have something in common, then." He paused and she tilted her head, wondering what on earth that could be. "We both faced death pretty early on. You got careful. I got cocky. Sometimes, I treat my life like I've had too much Tequila and I'm wanting a fight." He looked out the window across the lake. "I'm daring death to come at me again. Like this time, I'll be ready for it. Sky-diving, rock climbing…I even raced cars for a while."

"Maybe that's better than what I do. I treat death like it could win at any moment."

They stopped talking. Absorbing.

She accepted that Miguel did not try to hurt her—that he was hurting and trying to protect himself. Birk had helped her see that last night. What she didn't know was how they could go on from here. They had to work together.

"What are we going to tell Mr. Martin?" she asked. "I really can't afford to lose the job. I'm paying my mom's back mortgage."

"You're paying two mortgages right now?" he asked. When she nodded, he shook his head, but chose not to comment on her financial woes. "We go in on Monday and we get along. We show him a trophy that we'll pick up somewhere this weekend. They have trophy stores I'm sure, and maybe a certificate from the stationery store." He looked like he needed to sleep, like this was all catching up with him.

"*Can* we get along?"

"I respect you, Sera. I like you a lot. It's not going to be a hardship to make an effort to get along."

She nodded. "We both need some sleep."

He stood up. "I'm going to find a place to crash. Will you have lunch with me later?"

"I feel bad kicking you out of the cabin."

"I kicked myself out. It'll be good for me to deal with my consequences."

She smiled. "Okay. I'll see you at lunch then."

He leaned down to kiss her cheek. "I'll come to the cabin so we can walk to the buffet together. I don't want anyone gossiping."

She appreciated that. It was better if they carried on a little longer to save face.

Pride was in short supply today.

CHAPTER TEN

"I TOLD YOU IT WAS going to rain," Sera complained as they slogged down the trail. It wasn't rain, exactly. More like buckets being sloshed at them from all directions. The wind might have had something to do with that. It was miserable. Fucking miserable.

Miguel had hoped the weather would hold off so they could have a nice hike—but like everything about this trip, it didn't just rain, it poured.

A small clearing came into site, a cabin sitting in the middle of it. "Look, shelter." Thank God.

He was still surprised she came with him on the hike. He'd thought he was going to have to push harder. Turned out she was as eager to get away from everyone as he was. It was hard to keep up the pretense in public now that they were no longer fooling themselves.

He picked up the pace to the cabin.

"That might be somebody's house," she protested as he took the porch steps two at a time, thunder rumbling low and mean around them and echoing off the mountains.

"You want to stay out in this mess?" He looked in the window and knocked on the door. "Looks empty to me." He picked up the mat and found a key.

"What are you doing? Miguel, you can't just break into someone's cabin so we don't get wet. We'll stand on the porch until the rain stops or something."

He loved the look of incredulity. Her hair dripping. The hands on her hips. Was it less than a week ago it drove him nuts when she did that? Now the fact that she looked like a drowned rat about to school him turned him on.

He pushed open the door and peered in. "It's fine. Nobody will even know we were here." He pulled her through the door.

She freed her arm from his. "But what if they come back while we're still—" Her words cut off as her eyes widened in surprise. She made a slow circle. "What…the…what is going on?"

He closed the door behind them. The room was lit with dozens of candles, a small fire snapped in the fireplace, and the table was set with the good china from the camp dining room. The stuff they used for the catered weddings. A crack of thunder shook the cabin, the lightning strobing the small room three times. Hail pelted angrily at the windows and the music from the small stereo cut out sharply when another boom came. Good thing they didn't need power. Just shelter.

He reached for a towel by the door. "The storm is right over us. We got here just in time." He started dabbing at the water on her face, her eyes wide and confused. "We should get you out of those clothes before you catch a chill." He didn't know what a chill was, exactly. Maybe people didn't even catch them anymore. But it sounded old-fashioned and gallant, and he needed all the help he could get to turn this disaster date around.

"I don't understand what is happening here."

"We aren't breaking in."

She squinted at him. "We're not?"

Miguel led her to the fire and unzipped her hoody while he spoke. *"We* were told where the key was."

"We were?" Her t-shirt was soaked through too, so he lifted up the hem, but she didn't budge her arms to help, so he left it on her. "Explain."

He shrugged out of his own sweatshirt and draped it over the back of a chair near the fireplace to dry. "I didn't go zip-lining after lunch. Michael Tully brought me out here and helped me get the place ready. He came back out to light the candles while we were hiking in."

Sera shivered and relented when he went for her top the second time. "He hiked out here in the rain to light candles?"

"Nah. The cabin is accessible by road. It took him five minutes." Miguel took the blanket folded on the rocking chair and wrapped it around her shoulders like a cape. "Why are you not asking me what you really want to know?"

"You mean, why are you doing this?"

He settled her onto the rug in front of the fire, added another log, and snagged two glasses and the bottle of wine from the table. Sitting nearly cross-legged, which he was almost able to do now after a week of yoga, he poured the wine and thought carefully about how he was going to word what came next. "I did this for you."

"For me?" She sipped the wine and contemplated the flames as the logs popped.

"I'm going to use a lot of 'I statements' right now. It would be easier for me if you let me get them all out at once." He tried to ignore how uncomfortable his wet feet were, so he concentrated on how uncomfortable this conversation was instead. He'd never put himself out there, never wanted to, but this was one of those all-in things. You can't halfway jump out of an airplane. "Yeah. I thought I was being smart all these years, not getting close to anyone, but it occurs to me that I've been a coward. I know this marriage of ours is all make believe, but so is my whole life. Being at this camp with you—it's made me want to stop pretending. I'm not as okay as I lead people to believe."

He had her full attention now. Her big expressive eyes watching him expectantly.

"Hell, I'm not very good at this. Enough of the 'I statements.' I'm moving on to 'you statements.' Sera, *you* are smart and annoying and beautiful and sexy. *You* make me think about things I didn't know I wanted. *You* have burrowed so far under my skin that I hate to think about what I'd be if you left me. *You* are worth more to me than a week-long fling at camp. I'd like to see what happens if we keep going Monday. Well, maybe we could date for a while before we get the dog and the Prius. But that is the general direction I'd like us to take."

She blinked. Drained her glass. Looked into the fire. Finally looked back at him. "You did all this for me because you want to date me?"

"Well, yeah."

"I thought we agreed we were just going to work at getting along at the office."

"We should do that too. But after we talked this morning, I realized I still hadn't told you how I felt. I really like you. More than I thought possible. Do you like me?"

"I don't really know. You're too arrogant for one thing." When he didn't fight back, she carried on, "We don't have much in common. Other than we're employed by the same company. Hopefully we're still employed, anyway." She held her glass to him for a refill. "And you really hurt my feelings yesterday. I have spent my entire life protecting my heart. Figuratively and literally. You're not a risk I think I should take."

He stopped mid-pour. "Sera, you are the only person I have ever told about…my marriage. And I knew what I was doing when I opened up to you. I wanted you to know. I wanted you to understand that part of me because I don't show it to anyone else." Her lower lip did this little quiver thing that matched what his heart was doing inside his chest. "When I saw your scar, I did freak out. Because when I was a boy, I loved a girl and she died and it destroyed me. I don't know how I could survive if I lost you.

"Miguel—"

"Please let me finish. I was an idiot yesterday. I can't promise I won't be an idiot again, but it's not because I don't care. It's because I don't know what I'm doing."

"I don't know what I'm doing either," she confessed.

"Maybe we should just follow our hearts."

She rolled her eyes at his cheesy line. It was pretty bad; he'd give her that. "My heart is defective, remember?"

He grabbed her hand and kissed her knuckles. "It's not. It's strong—so strong it survived multiple surgeries." He squeezed her hand, thought of Howard and Lynn on the airplane, and went for it. "Can we try? Or have I ruined my chance at earning your trust."

The fire popped and she jumped. "It depends. What's under the domes on that table over there?"

"Sandwiches. I made them myself in the camp kitchen. And the coconut cake that they are serving with dinner tonight. I didn't make that."

"You made me a sandwich."

"I made you a sandwich."

She smiled but then shook her head. Shit, he could lose her here. "I'm scared."

"I know. Me too." *Please, just give me a chance.*

"But I'm tired of being scared. Also, coconut cake sounds really good. I'm a big fan of dessert."

"I've noticed." He reached over to move the wet hair sticking to her cheek. "There are marshmallows too, if you want to try your hand at those again."

She laughed as she walked on her knees to sit Yab Yum like they had yesterday, and he was instantly hard. How could he have missed holding her so much in just one day apart?

"I'm not really a good starter girlfriend, Castillo. You might have chosen someone a little easier to get back into the exclusive dating game with. Dating me isn't a walk in the park. I'm sometimes inflexible. I hear anyway."

As she wrapped the quilt around them both, he pressed his forehead to hers, feeling her everywhere. Feeling her in his breath, in his heartbeat. "You're the only one I want."

"I'm going to annoy you." She leaned back to look at him, his arms supporting her. He smiled and rested his head on her chest.

"I'm counting on it, princess."

They stayed like that awhile. The tension drained away. The world didn't matter. He just thought about how good it felt to hold her and the measure of their breath. He wanted to tell her he loved her, but it was too soon. She wouldn't believe it. Not yet. He'd have to just keep showing her. Every day. And then he'd tell her when she was ready to hear it.

Maybe Tuesday.

Her fingers tunneled into his hair as he kissed the skin above her bra. She sighed. The good kind. "So, we're just going to start dating when we get back? How does this even work?"

"You can brainstorm it all on paper and schedule me for a meeting to discuss it."

"You're super funny. Bring me a sandwich, Castillo."

They disengaged and she eyed the bulge in his shorts while he moved to bring over the food from the table. They both got out of their wet shoes and socks and stripped to their underwear while they picnicked on the rug in front of the fire. It felt easy. He had a feeling it wouldn't always be. But no sense borrowing trouble.

After food and more wine, she stood. "So, there's a bed over there."

"Fresh sheets and everything."

She pulled him up. "Is it my turn to lead?"

He'd have followed her back into the rain in his underwear if that's where she wanted to go, but luckily she stopped at the bed and directed him to sit.

Then she got on her knees.

Sera skimmed her hands up his calves, leaving goose bumps in her wake.

Up his thighs. Then back down. He thought his heart would stop when she made eye contact with him and cupped him through his boxer briefs. She was so beautiful it hurt to look at her. But when he reached for her, she evaded his grasp.

"You're going to have to trust me." She scraped a fingernail gently above the waistband. "I promise I won't take you anywhere you don't want to go."

Oh man. He was done for. All this time holding himself back. All his games. And he was done. The ice princess had him in the palm of her hand, literally now, and he was done.

She had him stand while she pulled down his underwear, then pushed him back down. She crouched low with a confident ease. Her hands were everywhere on his body except where he needed them the most.

He remembered the sweet sounds she made the other day. The way she tasted. He was harder than he'd ever been.

Miguel screwed his eyes shut. "If you don't touch me, princess…Oh Christ."

She didn't just touch him, she ran the flat of her tongue from root to tip and back down. "You'll what?"

He didn't know. He didn't know what she was asking. He didn't know the date, the year, his name. He knew Sera's mouth. He knew Sera's hands. He knew he wasn't walking out of this cabin the same man who'd entered it. He couldn't take much more. Not with his heart beating nearly out of his chest. Not with the heavy ache in his balls. Not with her mouth and her hands and …oh God…she rubbed her breasts on him. When had she taken off her bra?

Perfect pleasure. And a lot of it. She didn't seem to be tiring and he was getting close.

"Sera?"

"Hmm?" she hummed around him, the erotic vibration skimming pleasure across every nerve in his body.

"Oh God." That felt so good. A shower of sparks lit up the back of his eyelids. He was torn. If he asked her to do that again, he would come for sure. And everything inside him wanted to come. Now.

But no. "I need you. Up here. With me. Baby, please."

She sat back on her haunches again. Stood so he could rip her underwear down her hips. And then he tumbled her to the bed, grinding into her center but remembering the condoms in the bedside drawer. He bent to kiss her, long and deep, while his arm fished through the nightstand in search of the box. He knew he needed to break away, to get the condom on, but she was heaven and she was his and he was not a strong man.

The last of his willpower got him through the brief separation, got them protected, and then he was free to do what he so desperately needed. Inside her body at last, he paused, holding both of them still so he could look at her. Just look at her. And then he rocked into her slowly, slower than he thought he was capable of. But he wanted to feel her, take in every second of the bliss.

She arched her back and he took the offered nipple into his mouth. That set her off and she contracted around him, bringing him with her into the freefall.

They never made it back for the end of session party that night.

CHAPTER ELEVEN

Well, hell. She's wearing the pencil skirt again.

Of course, she was.

Miguel Castillo paused at her open office door. Not to leer. Not exactly.

Well, yes, exactly that. He was one hundred percent allowed to leer now. That's a perk of dating the same woman for two months. Leering privileges.

Sera was standing at the window in her office, talking on the phone. He'd come in to find out what was taking her so damn long sending him back her notes, but he didn't mind waiting for her to finish her call. It was a great view. Then he remembered she was supposed to get a call from the doctor's office today. All his muscles bunched up involuntarily and he watched her for signs of distress. Were her shoulders tense? Were her lips in that tight line she gets when she's upset and trying to keep it together? He couldn't see her eyes or the crinkle above her nose, and he didn't want to intrude or distract her. He had to wait.

What was he going to do if it was bad news?

Think positive, man.

Because, sure. Just thinking positive was totally going to make her heart okay if it wasn't.

He hated this. Hated not being able to fix her heart. At least literally. He'd been doing a pretty good job of taking care of it figuratively, if he did say so himself. She said she'd never been happier.

Had they jinxed her heart by being happy?

Now he was being an idiot.

Sera nodded and ended the call, startling when she turned to find him in the doorway. "Miguel."

"I know I don't have an appointment…"

She smiled and walked toward him, setting her phone on the desk as she passed. "It's fine. I'm fine. That was the doctor. I told you it was nothing to worry about."

All his bones turned to jelly. He was seriously close to losing all his machismo and falling down at her feet. "Well, that's good to know." He wiped what couldn't possibly be a tear out of his eye. "So quit slacking and get me that report. I've been waiting for it all damned morning."

She laughed. "I thought you wanted to brainstorm it together after lunch."

He picked up her hand, kissing the back of it quickly, wishing they hadn't decided on a strict no PDA policy at the office. "I thought you wanted to brainstorm it first by yourself on paper."

She leaned in, like she wanted a kiss. "Your way is not the only way."

"Neither is yours, princess."

A brisk knock at her door was followed by Mr. Martin saying, "Castillo, Worth, I need to see you in my office."

They exchanged quick, worried glances before following him. They'd been getting along fine. And they'd signed the love contract HR gave them two months ago. Everything was on the up and up. Well, Mr. Martin didn't know they'd pretended to be married on that trip, but that was no big deal.

They sat down and waited and waited and waited for Mr. Martin to say something. He kept looking at the piece of paper on his desk. He'd inhale like he was about to talk—and then nothing for long minutes.

"I had an interesting phone call this morning from Heather Tully, the owner of Camp Firefly Falls."

Had she thrown them under the bus? For what purpose? The Tullys had seemed more than fine with everything when they'd parted ways.

"What did Ms. Tully want, Mr. Martin?" Sera asked calmly.

He pulled out two envelopes from his desk drawer and slid them over. "Your itinerary is in there. Mandatory business trip."

Again, Sera could speak when Miguel could not seem to find the words. "I don't understand."

"They want Martin & Lewis Group to market their brand. It seems while you two were figuring out your differences over there, you impressed them. She said you knew how to sell the hell out of something and they want you. She said she'd never seen anyone work so hard at branding. You got the account. You're going back to camp."

EPILOGUE

Ten months later

CAMP FIREFLY FALLS OFFICIALLY STARTED its new season in two weeks, but Miguel and Sera had certain perks. One of them being that they got to come early and enjoy the scenery and brainstorm with the Tullys.

They could have stayed in the fancy lodge—which was turning into a true VIP venue, but they chose "their" cabin for the memories. Sera had been looking forward to this trip for months.

Miguel opened the door and ran into her when she stopped abruptly.

Almost a year ago, they had been awkwardly surprised by the idea of sleeping in one bed in the small cabin. She started to laugh. Really, nothing was ever going to be easy for them.

Their bed had been separated into two twins.

It became obvious from the layout of the room that the whole time they were there last summer; they could have just moved the bed apart into two. Which made so much more sense, now that she thought about it. How would the camp have accommodated single campers the rest of the season in double beds? It wouldn't have made sense to store and move single and double beds all summer depending on the session.

"If we had tried to be logical last year, we might not be together now," she said. "We wouldn't have slept in the same bed." Which started it all.

His arm came around her waist. "We would have eventually. Don't you believe in fate? Destiny?"

"Fate is not logical. So no."

"You wound me, princess. Are you saying you were not destined to be mine?"

She turned in his arms, standing on tiptoe to kiss his chin. "No. Destiny didn't choose. We did."

"You're such a romantic."

"You know what would be romantic? If you pushed these beds together while I go see about some different linens for it."

After sorting out the cabin, they went down to the lake. The weather was still chilly, but they took the canoe to Elephant Rock and back before meeting Michael and Heather for dinner at the lodge. They were helping taste test the new chef's dinner since they lost both the chef and pastry chef from last year to a Boston restaurant.

After an excellent mushroom risotto, Sera sat back in her chair with her wine.

"You look relaxed," Miguel said, kissing her cheek.

"I think I'm becoming an outdoor enthusiast. Or maybe just a risotto enthusiast. I love it here."

Heather poured more wine. "That's what we like to hear. Bring this glass with you, I want to show you something upstairs."

"Now you're starting to sound like Layla," Sera joked.

"Oh my gosh, did she hit on you guys too?" Heather asked. "She and her husband were both…adventurous…weren't they? They've tried Michael and I all three times they camped."

"Maybe you should add a Hedonist Week."

Heather's eyes lit up. "That might be fun! Maybe tomorrow we can google some naked people and find out more about how to market to swingers."

Sera loved that Heather was always up for anything. Though swingers' week might be too much.

Leaving the men at the table, she and Heather checked out the newly finished rooms. The rustic luxury of the lodge was really going to be an asset to them.

In one room, a gift bag sat on the bed. Sera's name on the tag. "What's this?"

"It's not from me. I'm just playing my part by getting you up here."

"Your part?"

Sera pulled out a box; inside was a dress. A fairly simple blush pink dress. The glance she gave Heather was answered with a "duh, put it on" look.

Heather handed her an envelope. "I have to go check on something." And she was gone before Sera could pin her down for more answers.

The envelope was a statement piece. Heavy and lined with foil inside. The card inside was written in fancy calligraphy.

Put on the dress. Come to the boathouse.

A fission of excitement bubbled in her belly. Miguel was up to something. She didn't care to guess, but probably she should wonder. And come up with the correct response. She hated being caught unaware.

Miguel had been the best boyfriend she'd ever had, surprising himself more than anyone else. He seemed to like being in a committed relationship. She'd gone into the whole thing knowing she'd have to give him room. Knowing that there would be bumps and she shouldn't overreact. And they had occasional arguments—but he hadn't wavered once since the night he took one plane to get away from her and one to come back.

She swallowed hard against the rising lump in her throat as she found the side zipper of the dress. It fit her well. It was old-fashioned. She felt a little like Baby from *Dirty Dancing* in it.

What was he up to?

They'd exchanged I love yous and condo keys before Halloween. He'd met her mom at Thanksgiving and introduced her to his family at Christmas. The Castillos had taken the Jewish thing pretty well and wrapped all her Christmas presents, of which there were many, in Hanukah paper. She wasn't going to quibble about it—they were sweet.

Things were going well for them. She didn't want to jinx it with thoughts of the future.

And she was sure he didn't want to either. This was just some romantic gesture he'd cooked up since they'd fallen in love here.

Relax, Sera. Count to ten.

There were shoes and a shawl next to the door of the lodge. She assumed they were for her—everyone else had scattered. So she crossed the lawn to the boathouse. It was alit with impossibly even more lights than last year. Heather had a thing for stringed white lights.

"Hello?" She walked further into the room and the music started.

Time of My Life.

Miguel stepped out dressed like Johnny Castle.

"Are you kidding me right now, Castillo?"

He grinned. "I know how much you like cheesy."

Sera started shaking. Every step that brought him closer made her quiver more. The weight on her chest had better be anxiety and not some kind of morbid heart attack.

Not now. Not tonight.

He stopped in front of her. He kept swallowing and he was shaky too.

"What's…" she had to clear her throat, "why are you holding a picnic basket?"

He opened up one side. She'd expected turkey sandwiches. Maybe s'mores fixings. Instead, a little fuzzy head popped up.

She choked and caught a bunch of girl feelings. "A puppy?" She lifted the little guy out and noticed a key fob attached to his collar. She brought the puppy to her chest and started crying. Why was she crying? "What's the key for?"

"The Prius."

She snuffled on her inhale. "You're giving me a puppy and a Prius."

Miguel nodded, reaching over to the scratch the puppy's chin. "I thought about taking you to Paris. Reenacting the proposal we came up with last year, but I didn't know a legal way to get you there without you knowing. And I wanted to surprise you even though you don't like surprises. But kidnapping seemed like overkill."

The puppy licked her face. "Oh."

"Oh?"

"I don't know what to say or how to react. I don't know what I'm going to do with a puppy right now."

"Did you not hear the proposal part?"

She pretended not to hear him this time either. The puppy wriggled. "He's so cute. Why did you give me such a cute puppy when it isn't practical—?"

"Sera, you can be practical about a lot of things. Loving me isn't one of them. I'm going to do this now. Don't hyperventilate." He got down on one knee. "Will you take me, the puppy, and the Prius and start the life we began dreaming about last summer? Will you marry me?"

Fifteen minutes ago, she worried that she didn't know the proper response. One minute ago, she'd wished he'd stopped saying proposal. She wasn't ready. He wasn't ready. They weren't ready. Now she knew the proper response, but could she say the words? "Yes. Yes, I'll marry you. And I'll even let you lead sometimes."

There went the laugh lines, the dimple, and his hand into his pocket to pull out a ring box.

She wondered if they came back to Camp Firefly Falls for their tenth anniversary, it would be free.

WANT MORE CAMP FIREFLY FALLS?

July 29: *Crushing on Cooper* by Violet Vaughn

When Allison Nelson's failed bakery leaves her career in limbo she takes a job at Camp Firefly Falls. It's a trip down memory lane to return to the camp she attended during her childhood, but she gets more than she expected. A corporate retreat arrives, and Allison is forced to sink or swim in a new romance with her first love. But a casual summer fling doesn't go as planned, and she dives in with her heart, even if she's too scared to tell Cooper about her son and a past full of failure.

Cooper Marshall spent the last decade as the golden boy of snowboarding winning multiple Olympic medals. When he decides to settle down and take a suit-and-tie job, he's sent on a retreat to Camp Firefly Falls. More than fond memories of the camp await him, and he discovers his childhood crush that got away. He makes the move he should have years ago, but Allison is not the Allie he remembers, and the weeklong fling she insists upon keeps him at arm's length. When her reason is revealed he must decide if he can take a chance on love.
www.campfireflyfalls.com

Aug 12: *Skinny Dipping Dare* by Zoe York

Navy SEAL Wyatt Henderson had signed up for a guys-only week of fishing and hiking and beer at his buddy's favourite camp in the Berkshires. Nobody said anything about campfire songs and kitchen duty and crafts at noon. Retro Throwback Week at Camp Firefly Falls is almost enough to drive him around the bend, and that's before the beautiful hippie in the girls' cabin next door decides he's no fun.

Tegan Bennett can't stand the insufferable, grumpy, gorgeous military man who wakes up every morning at dawn and takes up far too much space in her general vicinity. So when he throws down a dare, she takes it—and lobs him one of his own. It's on like Donkey Kong. Camp rules? Out the window. Along with her bikini top.

Is one week at summer camp enough to turn his frown upside down and tame her wild spirit? A lighthearted, sexy, opposites attract romp complete with a midnight dining hall ice cream raid.
www.campfireflyfalls.com

EXCERPT FROM *CRUSHING ON COOPER* BY VIOLET VAUGHN

~*~

My forks clatter in the pan I'm holding as I finish making the dessert. I think about the lake just yards away and decide to wander into the dining room to gaze out at it. When I do, I notice a guest at our adult camp walking down the dock. He's in swim shorts, and I have no doubt he's about to dive in. *Alone.* I huff in annoyance. One of the rules every guest hears upon arrival is that there is no swimming alone. This guy is blatantly breaking the rule, and I can't stand by and watch it happen.

I return to the kitchen in a hurry, and the pan I was holding thuds in the sink. The screen door that leads out of the kitchen squeaks open as I walk out. When I get around the corner, water splashes as the guy dives in, and my teeth grind as I clench my jaw. I can't exactly let him have it—he's a paying customer, after all—but I sure can make it clear this sort of behavior can't be tolerated. Our insurance policy won't allow for it.

I jog across the distance to get to the dock, and I'm breathless as my feet pound over the wooden deck. As I get closer to the guy, I notice his broad shoulders, and long arms are rippling with well-defined muscles as he strokes. He stops at the round inflatable float and holds on to it, which gives me my chance.

"Hey!" I yell.

The man turns toward me, and while he's probably fifty yards away, I can tell he's attractive. I call out, "You can't be out here alone!"

He tilts his head at me and then begins to swim back toward the dock. I take a moment to appreciate his fine form from this direction. He moves like an athlete, and my anger fades as he gets closer. I'll admit I'm a sucker for a hot guy. Especially since looking is all I get to do these days. When he gets to the dock, water splashes near my feet as he grabs onto the edge and lifts his face to me.

He frowns as I say, "I'm sorry, but—" *I know him.* Those blue eyes are burned into my memory for life. *Could it be?*

A grin covers his face, and he asks, "Allie?"

"Oh my god. Cooper?" A tingle rushes through me, because Cooper was the closest thing to first love a thirteen-year-old girl can have. He was also my brother's best friend, a year older, and so not into me. I soften with nostalgia, and my voice is calm when I say, "You're not supposed to swim alone. Our insurers don't allow it."

He lifts his hand and says, "Help me out."

I reach for him without thinking, and when his cool fingers wrap around mine, I realize my mistake. I try to jerk away, but Cooper's too fast for me, and he yanks hard. I lose my balance and let out a yelp before I fall in. I'm dressed in a white cotton chef's coat and the black-and-white-checked polyester pants I'm required to wear for work. The wet fabric clings to me as I come up for air. Cooper is laughing when I do.

I can't help it, and I laugh too before I say, "You haven't changed a bit."

Cooper glances down at my chest quickly, which makes me realize I'm wearing a bright-red bra under my shirt, and I think it's showing through the wet white fabric. He waggles his eyebrows as he says, "You sure have."

Considering the mosquito-bite breasts I had at thirteen require underwire now, I know what he means. And my cheeks heat as if I'm thirteen again. I splash water at him with my hand. "I can't believe you pulled me in."

He shrugs. "You said I can't swim alone, so I found a friend."

"Yeah, well, I'm getting out." The dock is firm in my hand as I tug myself over with the intention of hauling myself up instead of swimming to the ladder.

"Hang on, Allie." I turn to Cooper, and he says, "Swim out to the float with me. I'm not ready to get out yet."

Memories flood my mind. I was the timid girl who followed the rules, while Cooper was the complete opposite. He convinced me to do just about everything I ever got in trouble for as a child. But clearly I didn't learn a lesson, because I say, "Okay." I remove my shoes, and they thud on the dock when I toss them there.

I was a swimmer in high school, and even though my clothes are awkward, I have no trouble making it to the float. Cooper gets up first and reaches down to hoist me up easily, the way he used to do when I was a kid. I bounce on the inflatable trampoline as I land, and I push my loose strands of hair out of my face as I move back onto the sun-heated surface. Cooper lies down, and I do the same before I turn to face him. I say, "So."

Water drips down his tanned nose, and I glance at the full lower lip I fantasized about kissing for most of my teenaged life. "Fancy meeting you here," says Cooper. "You're the cook?"

"Pastry chef." Last winter, Cooper won several medals in the Olympics for snowboarding and retired from the sport.

But I think he's here with the pharmaceutical company, and I ask, "You're a corporate guy?"

"Not quite. I sell snow to the Eskimos." I frown at him, and he says, "New job. I'm in training to sell medical devices to surgeons."

"Oh." I blink as my brain tries to wrap around Cooper with a real job. "Congratulations on your Olympic medals. It was pretty amazing to watch."

"Thanks. You watched me?" Cooper's voice has lowered in tone, and it makes tiny hairs on my body stand up.

"Well, yeah," I say. "You're the closest I'll ever get to being famous. I told everyone I knew that you were my fir— brother's best friend."

He reaches over to move a strand of my hair off my face, and a tiny shiver runs through me at his touch. He asks, "Are you married?"

"No." My brain goes into overdrive as I imagine he's asking because he wants to date me. I picture us holding hands as we kiss by a campfire in an old fantasy that has almost become a real memory for me. I ask, "You?"

He shakes his head. "Boyfriend?"

"Nope." My heart doesn't care that this boy devastated us when he went off to prep school, and it reaches out for a guy I crushed on so many years ago. "You?"

Cooper lifts up to lean on his arm, and his body blocks the sun. He says, "No," before he lowers his mouth to mine.

Oh my god! His kiss is amazingly tender and does more than live up to my fantasies. While he only nibbles at my lips instead of diving in for more, my entire body heats up as if he flipped a switch. I'm pretty sure I hold my breath too, because I practically gasp when he pulls away to say, "No girlfriend either."

I chuckle at his joke and place my hand on my mouth to make sure this isn't a dream before I ask, "What was that for?"

"That was for all the years I kicked myself for not doing it the last summer we spent here. I swore if I ever saw you again, I'd kiss you before you could escape."

The grin covering my face almost cracks my cheeks. I'm thirteen again, and this time I'm not going to blow my chance. I'm not the timid girl I used to be. When Cooper leans down for more, I take all I can get. I open my mouth when his tongue darts between my parted lips, and I drink him in. He holds my face as if I'm a treasure while the muscles of his back flex beneath my palms. My fantasy of his kiss pales in comparison to the real thing. I think it might be the same for Cooper, because when we break apart, he smiles before he pulls me back for more.

www.campfireflyfalls.com

ABOUT THE AUTHOR

Gwen Hayes lives in the Pacific Northwest with her real life hero, their children, and the pets that own them. She writes stories for teen and adult readers about love, angst, and saving the world.

Gwen's first novel, *Falling Under*, was released in March of 2011 by NAL/Penguin and followed up by the sequel, *Dreaming Awake*, in January of 2012.

For more information about Gwen, please visit www.gwenhayse.com. In addition to writing, Gwen is a freelance editor at www.fresheyescritique.com.

She is represented by Jessica Sinsheimer of the Sarah Jane Freymann Literary Agency.

Made in the USA
Charleston, SC
09 July 2016